Her battle to leave home won at last, Emily arrived in London, to stay with her elder sister Melissa, and to start work at the Central Hospital – in the cardio-thoracic unit dominated by the world-famous but impossibly difficult heart surgeon Marcus Northiam. And Northiam's first assistant was James Leyburn, who as Emily knew had loved Melissa for years.

At the Central Emily soon fitted in to the hectic routine, quite unaware of the speculation aroused there by her occasional dates with James. She was so young, James reminded himself. He must keep an eye on her, make sure she was all right. Dear old James, kind as he'd always been, Emily told herself.

Meanwhile a storm was brewing at the hospital, resulting in an announcement from Northiam that rocked everyone. But that was nothing to the events at the hostel one night, that were to put Emily into the Central as a patient, her life in the hands of two surgeons – James Leyburn and Marcus Northiam.

Also by Elizabeth Harrison

And published by Corgi Books

Elizabeth Harrison

To Mend a Heart

CORGI BOOKS
A DIVISION OF TRANSWORLD PUBLISHERS LTD

TO MEND A HEART

A CORGI BOOK 0 552 10924 X

First published in Great Britain by Hurst & Blackett Ltd.

PRINTING HISTORY
Hurst and Blackett edition published 1977
Corgi edition published 1979

This book is set in 10-11 Pilgrim

Corgi Books are published by Transworld Publishers Ltd.,
Century House, 61–63 Uxbridge Road,
Ealing, London, W.5.
Made and printed in Great Britain by
Hunt Barnard Printing Ltd., Aylesbury, Bucks.

Contents

1. The Second-Rater

Silently, the electronically controlled doors opened. A small figure, green-gowned, stepped briskly through and over to the operating table under its glare of light, gloved hands raised chest high, as though about to pronounce a blessing – and a mind-blowing event that would be for the team awaiting him in the theatre. For this was Marcus Northiam, impatient and curt, who, when not concealed behind cap, mask and gown, looked – and behaved – more like an army general than the leading heart surgeon he actually was. Short-haired, with a clipped moustache, he was given to barking out his orders. To label him peremptory would be an understatement.

' 'Morning, Sister. Well, James, I hope you're ready for me. Eh?'

James Leyburn, Northiam's first assistant, was his opposite. Big and burly, he carried with him still, in his slow deliberate speech and tranquil unhurried approach to any problem, lingering traces of the West Country farming stock from which he came. Kindly and stable, he was the backbone of the unit, they all agreed. Northiam was the driving force, the innovator.

James Leyburn had already opened up the chest wall, and now, with Northiam's arrival, they moved on to the next stage of the operation. They had to put the patient on to the heart-lung machine, so that while they worked on his heart the machine would look after his circulation, keep him alive. The patient today was a London taxi-driver who without this surgery would have very few months left. Northiam and Leyburn were going to replace one of the valves in his heart.

Although the weekend of a late heatwave was nearly on them, the gallery was full. To watch Northiam doing an aortic valve replacement was a must, not only for undergraduates from the Central's own medical school but for postgraduates from all over London.

'Pulmonary bypass has now been established,' Northiam's clipped tones informed them. 'Mr Leyburn has just inserted, as you saw, the drainage cannula for the left ventricle. Now, in order to avoid the risk of bradycardia or fibrillation . . . ' Heads in the gallery craned forward, as everyone tried to follow both what Northiam was saying – even the physicians respected his clinical judgement in cases of valvular heart disease – and the highly involved surgery that was being performed.

At last they began work on the valve itself. With heavy curved scissors Northiam snipped away at its useless chalky leaflets, making room for the replacement.

'Right, that's it,' he said finally. 'Wash out. Hurry up, Mark.' Words and tone were amazingly like those of a busy dentist after a hard session with the drill. Today, though, in this theatre at the Central London Hospital, it was the heart that had to be rinsed free from any gritty particles dislodged by Northiam's surgical snipping. The saline solution gushed, and when the debris from the valve had been cleared James Leyburn began the prosaic routine of measuring the size of the opening now left, so that they could insert the new artificial valve.

'What have you got, James? Yes, I should say so. Let me just . . . yes, I think that's it. Now, where would that be, Sister?' He peered at the tray, and theatre sister's hand hovered. 'No, Sister, no, I don't think so. A little too small. That's more like it. Let's try this one for size, shall we?' They conferred, fiddled about, muttered together, took a good deal of time. For on the fit of this valve – a ring with a ball in the centre – the patient's future would depend. On its close fit and on the neat bit of sewing that would attach it to his heart.

While Leyburn held the valve steady for him, Northiam began to sew the ring to the heart itself, with about fifty

8

stitches, each one inserted in four separate positions – twice in the heart, and twice in the ring of the artificial valve. No blood must leak through. If it did, the operation would have failed.

Eventually, stitching almost completed, re-warming of the patient could begin, until, as the last stitch was tied off, James Leyburn removed the blood-supply tubes from the coronary arteries, followed by the clamp from the aorta itself.

'We are now preparing to terminate the pulmonary by-pass,' Northiam told the cramped population in the stuffy gallery.

Every head came forward.

'We shall transfuse the patient from the heart-lung machine until the central venous pressure reaches fifteen. How much blood do you estimate he will have received by then, Mark?'

Mark Corrie, James Leyburn's house surgeon, doing his best to keep up with Northiam's surgical demands, hesitated, went momentarily blank.

'Come on, come on, you shouldn't need to brood over it. Tell him, Sister.'

Sister never allowed herself to be ruffled by Mr Northiam, she always maintained, and in fact they played a well-recognised game of one-upmanship in the theatre, the state of play enthusiastically charted by her juniors. 'Do you mean in addition to the amount he has lost during surgery, sir?' she asked. 'If so, it would be between one and one and a half litres.'

'Information that should have been on the tip of your tongue, Corrie,' Northiam snapped.

A chubby and usually self-confident young man, in the theatre Mark Corrie could often be reduced by Northiam to a state bordering on stuttering idiocy. His value, though, could be measured in the fact that while he might, as he often put it himself, gibber, his hands never lost their dexterity. On this occasion, too, apparently imperturbable, he continued to assist without a visible tremor, though he had to force himself to concentrate on the readings that were being called out throughout the surgery from the batteries of machines monitoring the patient's condition.

At last the ultimate test came, and Northiam and Leyburn stood silent and waiting, their hands poised. Northiam's acute questioning glance, from almost lidless eyes, met the faded blue of Leyburn's, as they consulted together briefly, wordlessly.

For this was it. This was the moment to which these long hours in the theatre had been leading. Had the operation succeeded? Would the patient's own circulation take over now? Would his heart beat again, unsupported? Would the new valve function?

It would.

The taxi-driver had come through.

Another half-hour, though, was to pass before Northiam nodded to James Leyburn. 'Right,' he said. 'That's all, as far as I'm concerned. The rest is yours.' He turned on his heel, remarking 'Thank you, everyone, Sister,' to the air in front of him. A routine formula, no more. And then he was gone, in search of a cup of tea and a shower, while Leyburn completed the operation.

Even for Northiam, brusque to the point of rudeness as a way of life, it had been an unusually curt departure. But lately, partly, they thought, as a result of what the unit described as 'the great pacemaker row' – a more than usually furious encounter he'd had with the administration – he'd become much more moody and difficult. In fact, with every year that passed he seemed to grow more bad-tempered – and, they all had to admit it, more brilliantly skilled. He was perhaps the most famous, as well as the least popular, of all the surgeons at the Central London Hospital.

Nearly an hour and a half after Northiam's departure, James Leyburn nodded to the anaesthetist, who would take over the patient in intensive care. 'He'll do,' he said. 'I'm off now. I'll look in later to see how he's getting on.'

In the surgeons' rest room, beaded with sweat, he stretched wearily, swallowed a cup of cool stewed tea, and began checking through the roll of patients in the ward and in intensive care with Mark Corrie – new admissions, possible discharges, emergencies, changes in treatment. He'd been eight long hours in the theatre, and though he was a fit man, and used to it, he was limp with fatigue. He drained the last of the tea, and grinned at Mark. 'You did very well, you know. I don't suppose you enjoyed it much, but I can assure you that when he' – in the cardiothoracic unit this pronoun used without explanation inevitably meant one person, Northiam – 'when he starts demanding mental arithmetic as well as surgical support, you're in. It indicates that he has full confidence. Of course, he may not invariably make this one hundred per cent clear, I'll agree.'

Mark flushed. 'I felt like the village idiot.'

'You did well. Right, I'm off. Back about seven, I should say.'

For once, instead of running down to the ground floor, he waited on the wide landing for the lift. His tread was heavy. At this point all he wanted was to stretch out flat on a long couch with a cold drink, with enough free time ahead to be able to drop off to sleep. Half an hour would be enough. After that he'd be as good as new.

No chance. Instead he went out to the car park, started his Jaguar, drove out of the Central.

Of all times to choose, the bloody rush hour. He'd forgotten about it. But now he was faced with the necessity of driving through this lot to the station to meet Melissa's young sister.

As usual, Melissa was making use of him. Proceeding westwards from one traffic jam to the next, he had ample opportunity to dwell on this. It was nothing new. She'd been doing it for years – ever since her unforeseen announcement that she was going to marry Andrew Dunlop. Melissa had met him first in James's own flat, when Andrew, on a visit to London for an interview, had been staying overnight. It was a visit that landed him not only his present lucrative post with an oil firm, but Melissa too.

At first James had been incredulous. But he'd had to accept her decision, though he carried the scars to this day. And in the first years of her marriage, he'd leapt to answer any request she might take it into her head to make of him. Like some palpitating eager puppy, he remembered with self-disgust, anxious only to be received back into favour, seeing nothing else, overjoyed to find he still retained a place in her affections, he'd been grateful for every telephone call and accepted any demand on his time, however outrageous. He'd built vast castles in the air, indulged almost daily fantasies of seeing his lost love restored to him. Could she already be regretting her hasty marriage to Andrew? Had she found, so soon, that he had been no more than a passing infatuation?

James wore himself out in one long protracted effort to win her back. And this itself brought more conflict. Shame, too. He'd destroyed himself, week after week, as he'd swung back and forth, fighting himself every inch of the way. For James Leyburn had always believed in the traditional virtues. He was, as he often asserted, the squarest of the square, and he'd confidently believed that marriage to Melissa would be for his lifetime. For his, perhaps. But what about Andrew, his friend since boyhood? James knew he was spending most of his waking hours planning to make love to Andrew's wife, while his own future happiness was irretrievably bound up in the breakdown of Andrew's marriage. He hated himself.

A newly qualified house surgeon with a career stretching invitingly ahead when he'd first met Melissa, these years of struggle and despair had devoured his youth, until, free of her at last, he discovered himself to be middle-aged, with a promising future behind him, and ahead, nothing. No marriage, no family, no success. Simply Northiam and his whims. Day after day spent smoothing the path of an irascible surgeon of genius.

He shook his head, remembering the young James Leyburn and his overpowering love. What a gullible fool he'd been. Delusions about Melissa – for he could see now they'd been no more – had wrecked his career, destroyed his concentration when he'd most needed it, interfered with his time-keeping, blunted the keen edge of his developing skill. His surgical capability had slowed up. Only fractionally, admittedly, but the Central was a teaching hospital, and Northiam one of the leading heart surgeons in the country.

Standards were very high indeed. And what happened next was expected by everyone in the cardio-thoracic unit except James himself. Tom Rennison snatched the long coveted post of first assistant to Marcus Northiam from under James Leyburn's distracted eyes.

Rennison at that time had had everything going for him. Natural brilliance coupled with outstanding surgical skill – in those days it had been widely prophesied that he'd eventually become as famous as his chief. But then he'd come unstuck. At the Central they said he'd always taken too much for granted. A peer's grandson, he'd apparently assumed he could go his own way with impunity, had expected to be able to break the rules if he chose and get away with it. Sailing his brother's sloop one weekend, he'd been involved in cross-Channel smuggling, and as a result had found himself charged in the criminal courts. When the case came up, he'd been found guilty. Tom Rennison had gone to prison.

The hospital had been stunned – not into silence, though. For weeks they'd talked of nothing else. Say what you like, even in these anarchic days, the seniors said, this sort of affair shouldn't involve surgeons at the Central London Hospital.

After Rennison had completed his term of imprisonment there'd been no vacancy for him at the Central. The disaster had already given James his second chance. Northiam wanted a replacement for Tom in a hurry, and there was James, more or less waiting in the wings. But throughout the years he'd always recognised that his success had not been his own achievement but a side-effect of Rennison's personal tragedy. This knowledge stayed with him. In his own eyes he remained the understudy, the second-rate stand-in. Useful when someone fell out.

This was how Melissa regarded him, too. And here he was today, driving off to meet her young sister, despatched on the errand because Melissa had found something better to do.

In the train rattling through the London suburbs Emily – small and slight, in the new beige linen trouser suit her mother had helped her to choose, dark hair bouncing with every movement – peered left and right, shining-eyed, at drab rows of two-storeyed terraces. She must be nearly there. Her stomach tightened with apprehension, yet she'd never, perhaps, been quite so happy.

At seventeen she was on her own at last. She was arriving in London to stay with Melissa in Knightsbridge and begin her first job at the Central London Hospital.

Her half-sister, ten years her senior, was poised, fashionable, and led this sophisticated city life in a penthouse flat with huge sliding windows and panoramic views across London. On its doorstep were the extravagant department stores and the little chic boutiques that Emily had explored on one never-forgotten half-term holiday. Now, living in London herself, she'd be part of this scene, and companioned by the sister she'd admired from afar since babyhood. Melissa was blonde, and so beautiful it hurt, frail and lovely always in exotic floating silks, garlanded with clinking chains and long strings of translucent beads. Emily had always loved her.

In a flurry of anticipation she hauled her cases out as soon as the train drew up, lugged them behind her while she searched for a glimpse of her sister's spun-gold hair.

James spotted her at once, recognised Emily, the endearing little bridesmaid he'd somehow managed to look after on that day when he'd arrived at Wistaria Lodge, the Gorings' home in the West Country, wondering how in hell he was going to endure the celebrations. From the low white regency building, misty on that summer day with the drifting blue blossom, humming with bees, that had given the house its name, Melissa was shortly going to emerge for her wedding to Andrew.

James had not known how to bear it. However, if his heart was breaking, he had no intention of advertising the fact, and so, with apparent cheerfulness, he had devoted himself to the small Emily, and had, a good deal to his surprise, found her an adorable and comforting distraction.

He'd remained attached to her ever since. Over the years, to his relief, apart from growing steadily upwards, so that now she almost reached his shoulder, she'd hardly changed. Round-faced and soft-eyed, with the dark fringe he remembered, and the wide crinkling smile that had succeeded in lifting his spirits off the floor all those years ago. It could do so still, he found. At the sight of it, he took her in his arms and hugged her to him as though she remained that amazingly heart-warming infant.

She responded with enthusiasm equal to his. 'James,' she exploded. 'Super. Another person I know in London.' She'd always liked him, had longed for Melissa to marry him, anchor him safely in the family. But Melissa had scoffed. Boring old James, she had said, of course she could never marry him, he was simply tremendously useful, that was all.

And here he was explaining that as Melissa hadn't been able to get along to meet the train, he'd come instead. Obviously he was still being tremendously useful, though hardly, she recognised now, Melissa's type. With his burly frame and his plain gentle face, he looked more like one of the local farmers at home than a London surgeon from a famous hospital. Yet he'd been at the Central for ever, must be quite a personage there by now. 'I suppose,' she ventured cautiously, 'you're very senior these days?'

'Hardly.' He thought of Northiam. 'I'm just a very ordinary middle-grade sort of surgeon.' The exact truth, as he saw it.

Emily couldn't wait to impart her news. 'You know,' she burst out, 'that I'm coming to work at the Central, in the cardio-thoracic unit? On Monday?'

'Rumour had reached me,' he assured her with the encouraging look she'd almost forgotten, that seemed to come straight from the heart, honest yet gentle too, and that changed his face from its undeniable plainness to a sort of battered beauty. 'James,' she remembered the country doctor who was her father saying, 'has the gift of healing. Very rare and precious, and impossible to manufacture. Either it's there or it isn't. Mostly, of course, it isn't.'

'Do you think I'll be good enough?' she asked him now, her brown eyes searching his trustingly.

What was he to say? He looked at her blankly. She was so

shining and untouched, so glowing with hope, so devastatingly unaware of what was going to confront her, both in the hospital and under Melissa's roof. Unable to bring himself to puncture her eager confidence, he patted her shoulder reassuringly while his mind sought for words, rejected most. 'Of course, you may have a few teething troubles,' he said heartily, despising himself for a platitudinous bore, 'but you'll settle in all right, I feel sure of it.' He only wished he did. But he knew – none better, unfortunately – exactly how abominable Northiam was in the habit of being to his staff. He was used to it. He could take it. Day after day, if necessary. But this sheltered, vulnerable child?

She was babbling on excitedly. 'I'm only just out of secretarial college, you see. I've had no practical experience.'

James's heart sank. Northiam would make mincemeat of her in the first half-hour.

'Except in Dad's surgery,' she was continuing. 'In the holidays. I've worked in the office there since I was thirteen or fourteen, when I used to do the filing for them. And Dad has dictated a lot of his letters to me, for the last few months.' She was panicking now. Was her experience at home, in a family doctor's surgery in a quiet country town, worth anything at all at the Central London Hospital? Her father had, after a yearlong campaign of intensive propaganda on her part, eventually given in, found this post for her, in the hospital where he'd once qualified himself. 'Though I can't see why you won't live at home and help out in the surgery,' he'd grumbled.

'At least you must be thoroughly used to medical terms,' James was saying. 'You've no notion what a head start that gives you over some of them.'

'Dad has been dictating cardiology to me ever since it was settled that I was coming to the unit,' she assured him. 'And of course he has had his own ECG machine for years, so I understand all about T waves and base lines, all that stuff, and he taught me – when he first had it, ages ago – how to cut up the tracings and attach them to the case notes. And I – ' She stopped dead, flushed to the roots of her hair. 'I'm fearfully sorry,' she apologised, catching her lower lip and at

16

once looking, to James, about eight years old again. 'I'm boring on interminably.'

'Boring on.' Echoes of Melissa. How often, in the old days, exasperated, had she instructed him 'not to go boring on about that ghastly hospital for ever'. For the first time recently he'd entertained the astonishing possibility that what had seemed heartbreak might have been no more than a lucky escape. 'It sounds to me,' he told Emily, 'as if you're going to be a tremendous asset to the department. You'll soon find you can cope, I'm sure, and we'll count ourselves lucky to have you.' All of them, that is, except Northiam, if past experience was any guide.

'In a fluttery kind of way I'm actually rather looking forward to it,' she admitted, her eyes seeking his with a gleam of humour in their depths. She shook her hair back. 'I'll be thankful when the first week's safely behind me, though. And anyway,' her eyes lighted up at the thought, 'I'll be going home to Melissa and Andrew in the penthouse after work every day.'

'Yes.' James was curt.

Emily was annoyed with herself. How very tactless she'd been. He must care as much for Melissa as ever.

In the sudden silence they reached the Jaguar, and he stowed Emily's bags in the capacious boot, while she made a conscientious and determined effort to cheer him up. 'What a fantastic car,' she commented. It was immeasurably superior to her father's old Rover, almost as splendid, in fact, as Andrew's Mercedes. By now, too, his job must be the equal of Andrew's, though according to Melissa it hadn't been in the old days.

'You know,' she opened tentatively, 'I think you must be rather grand and important at the Central, whatever you say.'

As her soft brown eyes dwelt on him speculatively, James surprised in himself an unexpected longing to discover in their depths at least a hint of the glow that had been there when she'd spoken of going home to Melissa and Andrew. All he said aloud, and somewhat shortly at that, was 'Northiam's the one who's grand and important, as you're bound to find out very quickly. You'd better watch your step with him. It doesn't matter about me.'

They drove back through the thinning rush-hour traffic. 'Look,' James began. 'About Melissa. I haven't explained. She's not in Knightsbridge at the moment, that's why we're going the wrong way.'

A stranger to London's geography, Emily had had no inkling that they were heading in the wrong direction. 'I see,' she said politely.

'I'm taking you to St Anne's Square,' he explained. 'What we'll do is we'll go to my flat first, and Melissa will join us there.' Or so she had promised. He hoped she'd remember.

At this point Emily experienced the first faint niggle of doubt. James was frowning abstractedly, and Melissa seemed to have sunk without trace – was he impatient, wanting only to dump Melissa's blasted schoolgirl of a sister as soon as he decently could, go back to the hospital? Was she being an unmitigated nuisance to someone who, whatever he might tell her, was clearly very senior, and probably a highly distinguished surgeon?

He could see from her expression, no longer bright with excitement, but instead strained, uneasy, that she couldn't understand what was meant to be going on. Unfortunately that simply made two of them, and he hadn't the faintest notion how he was going to explain to Emily, who had always idolised her sister, that Melissa had probably forgotten all about both of them. And he hesitated to ruin Emily's first half-hour in London with ominous forecasts of the impending break-up of her sister's marriage.

His own reactions to the possibility had taken him by surprise, consisting, as they undoubtedly did, entirely of worry on Andrew's behalf. Friendship had outlasted love, unbelievable though this would have been a few years earlier. When and where had his love for Melissa died? He hadn't noticed its slow decline. All he knew was that it had gone, had seeped away through years of anguish into no more than the irritated affection he might have had for a young and exceptionally silly relative.

And now what was he going to do about Emily? Until she

had landed on him today he hadn't foreseen that she'd be a responsibility, hadn't expected to find himself so much involved in her future. Already, though, he was hating the thought of what she was likely to encounter in the next few weeks, wanting to save her from what lay ahead.

They drove into St Anne's Square, its lawns shaded by trees planted more than two hundred years earlier, while on this evening in early September water sprinklers caught the last of the sun in a fine spray of diamond droplets, and the country smell of sun-baked grass mingled with the city's exhaust fumes.

These gardens had been surrounded once by elegant Georgian houses with the tall sash windows and wrought-iron balconies of the period. Today, though, only two of these eighteenth-century terraces remained intact, most of the houses converted into staff flats for the hospital. At the far end of the square, a third and once similar row of houses was derelict. Several houses were missing altogether, demolished, and those remaining on either side were shored up by great timber buttresses, their windows blocked with corrugated iron. For nearly ten years – for as long as James had been qualified, in fact – there had been continual controversy and argument about the future of the row. Demolition orders had been followed by protests – from architects, the Georgian Society, the tenants' association – and preservation orders had been issued, compulsory purchase threatened, until most of the original residents had lost heart and moved away. Finally squatters had invaded several of the houses, while others had been boarded up by the council, and one had been taken over by the social services department for homeless or maladjusted children. The far end of this once prosperous square, in fact, had degenerated into a slum, and the remainder was for all practical purposes an annexe to the Central London Hospital. For on the north side, where a landmine one night in 1940 had demolished nearly ten houses, a staff residence – of flats and bedsitting rooms – with wide windows and brightly coloured panels behind concrete balconies and a faintly continental air had been put up by the hospital in the nineteen-fifties.

James, however, drew up outside one of the eighteenth-century houses, and led the way upstairs and into the sitting room of his flat. Emily was greeted by a sagging sofa, a low table littered with journals – *The Lancet*, *Thorax*, *British Heart Journal* – big comfortable armchairs with faded cretonne covers, and on one wall bookshelves from floor to ceiling, stacked with journals, textbooks and paperbacks. On a side table she saw a portable electrocardiograph machine, similar to one her father carried in his car to examine a patient's heart, a viewing box for X-ray films, and other pieces of apparatus she was unable to name. A friendly, untidy, workmanlike sort of room, she decided, unpretentious, but offering an unmistakable welcome.

James made for the telephone. 'I must ring across to the hospital,' he told her. 'Afterwards we'll have a cup of tea while we wait for Melissa.' His thirst was still with him.

'Couldn't I make the tea?'

'That'd be great. I'll show you.' He took her across the corridor, ushered her into a neat kitchen at the back of the house, and returned to the telephone.

Emily, more confident as soon as she was allowed to be of use, plugged in the electric kettle, found cups and saucers and milk, and looked out of the window on to the hospital buildings that dominated the skyline. No sign of Melissa, which was odd, but at least she herself had arrived here in London, and on Monday, in however lowly a post, she would be among the staff in those buildings, one of the people enabling this great teaching hospital to function.

The kettle boiled, she made tea.

James came back. 'I'll have to go over to intensive care fairly soon,' he informed her. 'So we'd better trot along and collect that dotty sister of yours first.' He drank his tea in great gulps, hurriedly, leaning against the draining board, pouring quantities of milk into it to cool it down. Anxious not to delay him, Emily did the same.

'Right,' he said, pushing himself off the sink unit, heaving himself upright. 'We'd better be off.'

He led the way out of the flat, set off with a loping, urgent stride right round the square to the dilapidated terrace at the far end. Here three houses were boarded up, while next to them two more houses, otherwise shabby, their plaster peeling, their balconies rusting away, had apparently been taken over by a squatter talented with a paint brush – both front doors displayed a meticulously executed peacock in full spread, their brilliant vivid colouring and air of eastern opulence at odds with the crumbling squalor all round. But the two peacocks were no more than a minor surprise. It was what came next that shattered Emily's precarious cool. James halted, put down her cases at the top of the area steps, and shouted for Melissa.

What's more, from within the revolting depths of the house, to Emily's stupefaction, came her sister's voice in reply. And then, with a flurry of long skirts, a clatter of platform soles, Melissa came rushing up.

'Em darling, you're here. At last. Gorgeous.' The rapturous heart-warming embrace, and the scent of musk, so different from her mother's lavender talc, were entirely familiar and reassuring. But what had become of Melissa's gleaming gold hair, hanging always so straight and heavy?

To her sister's stunned fascination, Melissa's small skull was covered in short corkscrew curls, cascading pinkly over her smart little head.

Emily stared, blinked.

It must be a wig. That would be it. Perhaps there was to be a pageant for the hospital – at home in Herefordshire this was a favourite form of fund-raising. And they must have caught Melissa in the middle of changing.

'Is it a wig? Are you dressing up? What for?'

From behind Emily came a stifled snort. James.

What had she said? Oh God, how awful. She flushed, scowled, and began again. 'Sorry, I – '

'Oh, Em, you are awful. Of course it isn't a wig, it's *me*, for heaven's sake. Don't you like it? Do say you do.' She ran long fingers through the soft springy curls, gave Emily a slanting gleam of gnomish enquiry. Under the pink mop her green eyes were mysterious and her features seemed to have taken on strange new lines and curves.

To James she looked depraved. Unbalanced, too.

She picked up his reaction instantly. 'James hates it, I can see.' She smiled enchantingly at him, confidently awaiting his hasty denial.

It failed to come. The smile would have worked on him once, he knew, but today it triggered no response except impatience. 'Are you ready?' he asked, glanced at his watch. 'If you want me to run you back to Knightsbridge you'll have to come now. I must be back in the hospital inside half an hour.'

Melissa sighed. 'Always that wretched hospital. If only you could relax now and again.'

James tapped a foot on the pavement. '*Now*,' he said.

'Darling, I'm simply not ready to depart like this in one mad rush. I'll tell you what, don't you bother. Em and I can get a taxi.'

He hesitated. 'Emily's had a long journey, and she's pretty tired, if you ask me. It's getting late, too. Don't you think –'

'I'm perfectly all right.' Emily was aghast. 'And it isn't a bit late.' Did he think he and Melissa had an exhausted toddler on their hands, or what? Furious, she glared at him, brown eyes sparking.

'Of course it isn't.' Behind James's back Melissa pulled the conspiratorial face she'd so often used in the past when their parents were being unreasonable.

'Off you go, James,' she said firmly. 'Over to the hospital this minute. Em and I can manage very nicely without you, thanks very much all the same.'

'Just as you like.' He was short, and walked away up the square with no further comment.

Emily felt dreadful. He'd been so kind, meeting her and giving her tea and everything. But Melissa only made another rude face at his retreating back. 'What an old *stick* he's turning into,' she said. 'No need to take any notice, though. You aren't really tired, are you?'

'No, of course not.' Emily, indignant still, repudiated the possibility at once, but her eyes followed James as he walked along the square and up the steps to his own house. She pulled herself up sharply. No need to feel suddenly as if London was empty, and she herself alone. She was standing here talking to Melissa, and they were going to take a taxi across to the penthouse in Knightsbridge she'd been so much looking forward to seeing again.

'Darling Em,' Melissa hugged her again. 'I *am* so glad you're here.'

Emily felt better at once.

'Even if it is the tiniest bit complicated this evening.'

Emily's stomach contracted. Was she in the way here? Didn't Melissa want her? Was she nothing but a nuisance all round?

'Come along in, anyway. I'm dying to tell you about everything.'

At least this sounded more helpful. But what were they going to do in this slum?

'We haven't much time, though.' Melissa's sweeping skirt of Liberty silk printed with a pre-Raphaelite design descended the area steps. 'We're going to have a party. The others have gone off to collect food and drink.'

The area smelt of dampness and dustbins. Melissa, talking volubly, pattered blithely through into a basement kitchen, sat down at a table covered in what looked like junk. 'Come along,' she urged hospitably, almost proprietorially. 'I've masses to tell you, and we haven't long.'

Emily dumped her cases, looked about her. 'What are you doing here?' she asked baldly. A dirty barred window faced on to the area, a sink beneath it was piled with washing-up.

Ignoring the mess round about her, which was customary, Melissa put her elbows on the table, ran her fingers lovingly through her pink curls, and as usual began in the middle. 'This is Greg's pad,' she explained unhelpfully. 'You'll adore Greg. He's the greatest.'

'Greg?'

'Yes. He – oh, you'll see for yourself.'

'You mean he *lives* here?' Emily's shocked brown eyes traversed the peeling walls, the cobwebbed ceiling, the grimy window.

Melissa pulled another of her conspiratorial faces. 'Of course it's a bit of a slum, but Greg doesn't mind that. He specialises in problem children, you see, and he says living here brings him much nearer to them. This is what they have to face all their lives, he says – he's absolutely *dedicated*. And he thinks Knightsbridge is *unspeakable.*' She smiled, like a proud yet at the same time humorously tolerant mother. 'Central heating, washing machines, mixers, hoovers, floor polishers – Greg loathes them all. According to him they're a pathetic middle-class shelter from reality. And they're destroying our souls.'

Certainly Greg had seen to it that his own soul was in no danger from modern household appliances. The basement lacked even a gas stove. Only the big old Victorian range stood in the hearth, rusted, ash spilling from it, and a group of Camping Gaz tripods and cylinders scattered around it – presumably these particular kitchen aids were not on Greg's index.

And now outside on the area steps there was a hubbub. A crashing and the clatter of feet, raised voices, a sudden burst of laughter, a snatch of the latest hit from the top of the pops – and into the basement, flowing round Emily, transfixed, as though she were a piece of furniture, came a horde of tall strangers in blue denim, arguing vociferously.

With them came a pungent aroma of barbecued chicken. Several greasy parcels thudded on to the table, accompanied by a transistor tuned to Capital Radio, a big carton of crisps and two litres of wine.

Melissa was on her feet. And then she disappeared into the blue denim, and Emily could see only her long fingers, white at the tips, pressed rapturously into a pair of thin shoulders belonging to what looked like a lamp-post in shabby jeans, surmounted by a head of glinting gold.

To Emily, trying not to stare, not to fidget uneasily, they seemed to cling together for ever. Around her everyone else talked and argued, apparently unaware she was there at all.

She wished she wasn't. James would have taken her to Knightsbridge, he'd offered to. If only she'd gone with him.

At last Melissa broke away. 'Greg darling,' she announced. 'This is Em. She's arrived.'

Did Emily see, or imagine, the brief surreptitious moue of boredom Melissa sketched in Greg's direction? Before she had fully registered it – whatever it was – blue eyes that had been devouring her sister turned momentarily, unseeingly, on Emily. A wide mouth spoke. 'Hi,' it said genially. 'You've joined us. Great. Meet Emily, you lot.' The blind blue gaze returned to Melissa.

Nothing had prepared Emily for Greg. For if his pad was a slum, he himself was the most handsome man she'd ever met. Thin and brown, long-limbed, with classic chiselled features, his hair a helmet of burnished gold and eyes as blue as the sea.

While Emily rocked on her feet, the wine was poured and the party began.

2. Melissa in Knightsbridge

The next morning Emily woke when Carmel, a pretty West Indian girl in her early twenties, whose room she'd apparently occupied, announced cheerfully that she'd come off night duty and proposed to go to bed. Now. In the only bed the room held. Emily leapt hastily and apologetically out of it, rolled up the shabby sleeping bag that Greg had found for her, while Carmel placed her own sleeping bag on the low camp bed. Luckily, she seemed not in the least put out to find Emily in residence, simply warned her that she intended to go to sleep at once, so that if Emily wanted to remove her scattered belongings from the room, would she either do so immediately or not until around five in the evening. Hurriedly hurling her possessions back into her case, Emily explained that she'd be going back to Knightsbridge with her sister quite soon.

'Your sister? You mean to say that Melissa is your sister?' Carmel made no attempt to disguise her amazement. 'Well, what do you know?'

Emily, dressing fast, thanked Carmel for the use of her room overnight, hung her beige jacket over her shoulders and made for the door.

'Feel free,' Carmel said, zipped up her sleeping bag, and appeared to drop off instantly.

The house was quiet around her as she went downstairs, and Emily imagined that perhaps she had overslept hopelessly. Where were they all? She continued on through the hall and down the basement stairs towards the big kitchen, in search not only of Melissa but of breakfast. The all-pervading silence began to unnerve her, though, so that she found herself creeping softly down the final flight.

She opened the kitchen door cautiously, peered in.

No one was up. But there, on the rickety old couch, was Melissa's cascade of pink curls, half lost in the pillows, and next to it, mingling gold with the pink, was a blond head.

Greg.

Very quietly indeed, Emily shut the door. Open-minded, unshockable, she had supposed herself to be, and certainly fully prepared, in theory, to discover that her sister, married ten years, was having it off with someone other than her husband. But theory and practice turned out to be worlds apart, and in reality, though this was the permissive age and she, surely, part of it, she was shattered to come on her sister curled up in bed with anyone but Andrew.

Indecisively, she retreated up the basement stairs, into the empty hall.

After all, it was nothing to do with her, was it? And she'd seen for herself how much in love Greg and Melissa were. Their behaviour was natural, normal, acceptable. Some childish inhibition, some odd hang-up that until now she'd known nothing about, must be at work in her to cause this upset. Because she was upset, no good pretending she wasn't. But what cause for alarm could there be in the sight of two unmarried – or at any rate unmarried to each other – human beings in bed? Any abnormality must be in herself. She was being hopelessly prim and naïve. People were doing this all the time. She took a deep breath to steady her nerves. She'd been taken by surprise, that was it. London was not darkest Herefordshire, after all. And Melissa had always been a trend-setter. Though perhaps this could not exactly be described as setting a trend?

But what was she to do now? Recovering from what she now considered to be her first puritanical shock, she un- earthed another much more familiar sensation. Hunger. Long past breakfast time – but what was she meant to do about it? Surely they didn't expect her to go into the kitchen and start preparing it? Or did they? Her cheeks grew hot. She couldn't do it.

27

She'd have to hang about until they woke up.

Hang about where?

The derelict house remained unhelpfully silent around her.

Impossible to return to the attic bedroom where she'd spent the night. Carmel was already asleep there. Emily stared round the shabby, dirty hall, seeking inspiration. it failed to visit her. 'Pull yourself together, Emily Goring,' she told herself fiercely. She'd assured her parents, week after week, tediously, that she was fully adult, overdue for independence. She'd come to London, by her own decision, to earn a living. So what was she doing, skulking in the hall like this, panicking because she'd discovered her sister in bed in the kitchen with Greg? What had become of her self-reliance? Her sense of adventure? London was around her. The morning was hers, she could do exactly as she liked. She was entirely free, no parents were waiting for her at home. 'Lovely,' she assured herself experimentally.

The trouble was, it didn't feel lovely at all. Instead, unwelcome pangs of homesickness demoralised her, a maddening longing, irrepressible, for Wistaria Lodge and the friendly kitchen there. Gas stove, refrigerator, coffee percolator, pop-up toaster.

She couldn't go on like this, hovering in the hall, afraid of the street outside. She must take a grip on herself, and go out.

She opened the big front door, winked at the gaudy peacock, and went down the dirty steps. St Anne's Square was shaded and cool at this hour, and she enjoyed walking through it. Wandering on round the corner, she found herself in the hospital.

The original medieval hotel dieu that her father had told her lay hidden in an inner cobbled yard was out of sight behind the main eighteen-century building that confronted her, with its two highly ornamental Victorian Gothic red-brick wings. Squashed in round about as needs and funds dictated was the twentieth century's somewhat muddled contribution, saying – according to Emily's father again – very little for this era's sense of beauty or proportion.

She could see what he meant. But the modern tower block – the surgical block, where she'd be working – and its trail of sheds and garage-like excrescences spoke to Emily of her own future, and it was with a surge of renewed hope and joy in the day that she walked between the buildings. Everywhere people were hurrying, pushing trolleys piled with metal containers or laundry baskets, delivering papers or mail or soft drinks. Others stood about arguing over lists, laboratory workers in stained white coats strode clinking about with crates of test tubes, nurses in pastel stripes and fly-away caps whisked round corners, while everywhere she saw tall young men in blue jeans and preoccupied girls in cheesecloth shirts and more blue denim.

This was a blow. The beige trouser suit had been a mistake. Denim was in. She would have done better in her old jeans, she thought regretfully.

Suddenly she came across the car park, spotted James's Jaguar, a little dusty in the morning sunlight. For some reason, this restored her sagging self-confidence, and, cheerfully in search of breakfast, she turned away from the hospital into a bustling little shopping street. No need to hang about hungrily until Greg and Melissa were up. She'd eat out. Emancipation was breakfast in a coffee bar near the hospital.

After coffee, toast and marmalade in the Black Sheep, she went back to the hospital, with the idea of becoming familiar with the whereabouts of the various departments. She kept a keen look-out for James, too. What fun if she ran into him – he'd almost certainly spare a few minutes to show her round. No luck, though.

By the time she returned to the crumbling house in St Anne's Square, it was well after eleven in the morning. Halting doubtfully at the top of the basement stairs, she was relieved to hear voices.

Evidently just up, Greg and Melissa were drinking Nescafé and eating Ryvita spread with honey at the big table. They invited her to join them.

'I've had breakfast. In a coffee bar. I've been out for hours.'

Melissa was put out. 'What on earth did you want to go out so early for? You could have waited and had breakfast with us.'

'I wanted to explore,' Emily, who by now had forgotten her earlier homesickness, told her sister enthusiastically.

'Oh, Em, you must be mad. Explore this dump? Never mind, have a cup of Nescafé, an then we'll go over to Knightsbridge for lunch. Greg says he's got to go out in a minute. Isn't it a bore?'

At last they were on their way across London – by bus, at Emily's insistence. Ignoring Melissa's pained protests, too, she'd climbed the stairs to the top deck, and now, peering down on the famous shops of Piccadilly, on the trees and deck chairs of Green Park in the September sun, she assured her sister, for what seemed the twentieth time, that her lips were sealed.

Melissa, clover-pink curls fluffed up round her face, fresh and charming in the long flowered skirt she'd worn the previous evening, and a clinging lacy top that revealed a good deal of silky brown skin, remained urgent.

'You do see, don't you, Em, why you mustn't breathe a single word at home?' she reiterated.

'I've said I won't if you don't want me to.'

'It's fearfully important, though. I must be able to rely on you not to mention Greg, ever.'

The bus reached Hyde Park Corner, pulled up to allow a troop of cavalry to trot across the traffic and into the park. Emily's eyes followed them as, red plumes tossing on high helmets, harness jangling, and horses shining with health and grooming, they clattered over the road, while she assured Melissa somewhat absently-mindedly that she wouldn't utter a word.

'Do *concentrate*, Em.' Melissa was sharp. 'Stop gawping like a tourist. You can see the Household Cavalry any day. Listen, this *matters*.'

The bus, apparently in league with her, jerked and moved on, round the corner and along Knightsbridge. Horses and riders slid out of view.

'Now don't go and forget, will you?' Melissa urged. 'And don't tell them at Wistaria Lodge, either. I don't want anyone to know about me and Greg. Understand?'

The bus turned the corner into Sloane Street, she picked up her raffia basket and Emily's small overnight case, gathered her long skirt. 'This is our stop. Come on.'

The entrance to Oriel House could hardly have been more different from the Georgian terraces of St Anne's Square. Here there was dark charcoal-coloured brick, jutting plate-glass windows with stainless-steel frames. Inside, they walked on tawny carpet thick as autumn leaves, between cork-panelled walls, where spotlights were trained on to wide concrete saucers brimming with greenery – rubber plants, palms drooping gracefully, something that looked to Emily like a miniature fig tree, spider plants, philodendron, cissus, round the rims variegated ivy trailing down on to the tawny carpet. They walked past and into a walnut-panelled lift that, hissing and sucking, wafted them up six floors in as many seconds.

In the penthouse they were greeted by space and order, a kitchen Greg would have hated, full of gadgets, and a cross Italian housekeeper, black eyes snapping.

'You did not let me knaw, Signora. I not knaw at oll what 'ad 'appened to you and ze Signorina both. I was zo worried.'

Not worried so much as furious, Emily saw at once.

'I told you we were going to a party, and not to wait up, Anna.' Melissa was surprisingly placatory. 'My sister was keen to stay on, you see, until the end.'

Emily's eyes widened. *She* had been keen to stay on?

'Eef you not coming 'ome at oll, I zort you telephone. What I suppose to tell ze Signor when 'e ask?'

'Did he telephone?'

'Naw. Bot eef 'e 'ad, what I to tell 'eem?'

'Well, I'm sorry. It was late, you know, and I thought you'd realise what had happened. Now we'd like some lunch.'

'Bot you take ze Signorina to lonch at 'Arrods, you tell me.'

'Well, I've changed my mind. It's too late. What can we have?'

'Zere are ze escalopes for zis evening only. Bot you 'ave zem now, and what you eat for deenair? You 'ave not zort. Ze Signor, 'e weel want – '

'Yes, I know. Never mind. We'll have the escalopes now. You can get something sent in for this evening. There's all afternoon, after all. We'll have lunch on the patio, as it's such a lovely day. Come on, Em. We'll have a drink while we're waiting.'

Melissa crashed through the swinging doors separating the shining great kitchen from the vast living room, waded through a wide expanse of off-white shaggy carpet, and stepped out of the tall sliding windows on to the patio, high above the roar of traffic.

Like the living room, the patio was L-shaped, stretching round the corner of the block, facing both south and west, catching all the sun there was. It was plain, now, how Melissa acquired her becoming tan. Today the awnings were up, chairs were scattered invitingly, a gaudy swinging couch, too. A brilliant umbrella shaded a round white table, and the day, airless and heavy in Sloane Street, was cool and refreshing, with a soft breeze here that ruffled the petunias – purple and pink, spilling out of more of the concrete saucers they'd seen in the hall.

Melissa flopped on to a long chair, tilted the umbrella with a practised hand to protect her face. 'Bloody woman,' she complained. 'God knows we pay her enough. And you see how it is, she can barely be civil to me. All that carry-on simply because I forgot to telephone last night, or give her advance notice we'd be here for lunch. Who does she think she is?'

Swinging on the gaudy couch, Emily pondered. 'We pay her enough,' clearly referred to Melissa and Andrew. On her previous short visit to the penthouse she had failed to realise the complicated life her sister led. Parties in St Anne's Square, with Greg, then back home to Andrew and a bad-tempered Italian housekeeper. Emily was impressed. It had never occurred to her that, outside television drama, real people –

let alone her own relatives – actually led existences like this.

Melissa kicked off her shoes, wriggled her toes, stretched long and sensuously. 'Be an angel, Em, go and fetch the drinks trolley. Wheel it over here, and I'll make you a concoction. We can both do with a drink.'

In the great living room Emily found the smoked glass and chrome trolley, clinked it carefully over the shaggy pile and out to Melissa.

'Oh, you are sweet. A long drink, I think, don't you? A lovely long cold drink.' She peered suspiciously into the ice bucket. 'Ah,' she said. 'At least she's remembered the ice today. How about a Pimm's?'

'Super.' Pimm's was not a drink provided by Emily's parents, who took to iced lemon tea in hot weather. Pimm's, Emily was fairly sure, had gin in as well as all the greenery. It was very much a Melissa and Andrew in the penthouse touch.

'Pop in and ask Anna for mint and cucumber, would you? I really can't face her just yet myself.'

The Pimm's was followed by a delicious lunch – provided, however, by a disapproving Italian lady in an unmistakable huff. Unfortunately, though, with each mouthful Emily took it became easier to forget the huff and the fact that she was eating what had been intended for Andrew's dinner.

'Where's Barnaby?' she enquired, halfway through the meal. She had expected him to lunch with them, had supposed the penthouse would be ruled by his needs and demands. 'He's walking and beginning to talk,' Melissa had told her on the telephone only a week ago, 'and there's no holding him.'

Now, though, she shrugged impatiently. 'Thank heavens, he has his lunch with Joan earlier. He's resting now. Otherwise it would be impossible to have any peace. He's adorable, of course, Andrew will tell you. But totally exhausting.'

The housekeeper returned with superb black coffee, and Emily was thankful for it. What with the Pimm's and the food, following a party that had gone on until four in the morning, she could easily have gone to sleep in her chair. But the coffee revived her and, the Pimm's having removed a few inhibitions, she began to cross-examine Melissa about her hectic love life.

'Are you and Greg having a full-scale affair?' she asked. 'How long have you known him, anyway?'

'I told you –'

'It's all right, there's nobody around. You must tell me all about you and Greg. Please, Melissa. I'm dying to know.' During the bus ride this vista had preoccupied her quite as much as the shops in Piccadilly or the Household Cavalry.

Melissa gave one of her disarming, rueful grins, pushed the pink curls out of her eyes. 'Oh, darling,' she protested. 'You are awful. Always wanting to know everything.'

'Well, but tell me. I mean – last night. Was it the first time?'

'No, of course it wasn't. Greg and I – we – oh, I don't know. I can't explain.'

But since Emily was determined that Melissa should explain every detail – how was she going to leave Wistaria Lodge behind in the past, turn herself into a mature and sophisticated city type, unless her sister came clean? – and Melissa had for weeks been forced to bottle up both her excitement over Greg and the general awfulness of the staff in the penthouse, suspecting her, she was sure, of hideous crimes, and loyal to Andrew to a woman, it was not long before the dam burst. Emily, vibrating with excitement, was treated to a minute-by-minute account of Melissa's first meeting with Greg, their subsequent rapturous love, and their almost daily meetings since.

Emily was deeply moved. However, her common sense – a quality that, unlike her sister, she possessed in full measure – warned her there were pitfalls ahead.

'What about Andrew?'

Not a question Melissa was prepared to encourage. After all, it was not to hear this sort of thing that she had put herself out to tell Emily so much about her relationship with the handsome, intelligent, soulful, and fantastically handsome Greg.

'Nothing to do with him,' she said shortly.

Emily couldn't agree. 'But, after all, he *is* your husband,' she pursued relentlessly.

'I'm dreadfully fond of him,' Melissa said. The phrase tripped out meaninglessly, as if she had learnt it by heart months back, and now didn't trouble to listen to it herself. Her eyes velvety with love again, she returned to her theme, her soft dreaming gaze slipping past Emily into the distance. 'I can't tell you how extraordinary it is, Em. To find the one person at last. The *only* person. All the problems simply drop away, vanish into nothing.'

No problems? Even at seventeen Emily doubted this.

'But Andrew – '

'Oh, Em, don't keep on. He mustn't find out. That's all there is to it. So you must be fearfully careful and say nothing. Ever.' She sat up, felt for her sandals. 'Now I'm going to have a bath. You can have the bathroom after me, if you like, and use my bath oil and my toilet water. I've a hair appointment at four, so you'd better amuse yourself this afternoon. Go along to Harrods and browse.' She glanced at her watch, a flat gold disc that Emily remembered Andrew had given her a couple of birthdays back. 'I'll have to rush. I'll call you when I've finished in the bathroom. When Andrew's away you can use mine, but when he's here you'll have to use the nursery one.'

Melissa's bathroom, leading off her cool coffee and cream bedroom, had been done over since Emily's visit, when, as bleached and fresh as the bedroom, it had been panelled in pine, with white fitments. Now the place was onyx and gold, and the bath had become an oval across one corner, surrounded by vistas of bronze mirror-glass. Emily lay luxuriously, twiddling the gold taps with her toes from time to time, and thinking about the golden Greg in his basement slum a stone's throw from the Central.

Thinking about the hospital, of course, at once brought another figure to mind. Neither golden nor godlike. James. And considerably to her surprise, as she dried herself on the thick beige towel Melissa had left her, drenched herself in her sister's toilet water, it was James who took possession of her thoughts while she put on what, until today, she had imagined to be her best evening skirt, and prepared to sample the joys of Harrods.

Before she left the penthouse, though, she went in search of Barnaby. She was fond of her small nephew. The Italian housekeeper, still cross as two sticks and busy cutting out pasta, presumably for the reorganised evening meal, informed her – clearly with some pleasure – that she was too late. The bambino – the povero bambino, for some reason – had been taken by his nurse to play in the square for the afternoon.

However, when Emily returned from what – after a quick glance at a few prices – had been an afternoon of window-shopping, Barnaby and Joan were back, and she joined them for nursery tea. No sign of Melissa, but Andrew, who had been in Scotland all the week, appeared as they were finishing the meal.

Barnaby shrieked with joy the moment his father's head came round the nursery door. 'Daddy, Daddy, Daddy,' he yelled at full pitch, scrambled to the ground, hurled himself across the room and into Andrew's arms. The two heads were facsimiles. The shape of Barnaby's skull, his dark hair and intelligent eyes – Andrew in miniature. It was soon plain, too, that father and son formed a well-established mutual admiration society. Once Andrew had joined them, no one else counted with Barnaby, and after a hilarious time rolling about on the floor together and yelling blue murder, he left the room enthroned on his father's shoulders, gabbling excitedly. Andrew told Joan to help herself to a couple of free hours. He'd bath Barnaby himself, and tuck him up for the night, too.

Emily would have liked to join the bathing party, but saw she'd be an unwanted extra, so instead she went out on to the patio, sat down on the gaudy swinging couch, and turned the astonishing pages of Melissa's *Vogue*. Her mind wasn't on it, though. She felt an uneasy sense of disloyalty – but to whom? Melissa? Barnaby? Andrew? To all of them. They were skating on thin ice, and she as much as any of them. At any moment something might give. The surface would crack. What then?

At dinner that night her brown eyes dwelt wonderingly on her sister who, magical in floating diaphanous gauze drifting above green harem trousers and flimsy gold sandals, was flirting outrageously with her husband.

Melissa's clothes alone, the afternoon's window-shopping informed Emily, must have cost her sister – or, to be accurate, Andrew – one hell of a packet. The pink curls cost money too, though two hours in Knightsbridge had given Emily a new angle on pastel-coloured curls, as common there, it seemed, as blue denim in the Central. Now, newly shampooed and set, clustering close to her head, they gave Melissa a weird fascination, and Emily suddenly understood that her sister, who looked to her this evening half witch, half urchin, was in fact wholly seductive, easily able to hold both Andrew and Greg in the palm of her hand and play them as she would. James too, no doubt.

The realisation was curiously depressing, and Emily's self-esteem wilted. Her own clothes were provincial and school-girlish. The pretty cotton skirt she'd chosen with such certainty to see her through many London evenings looked frumpish even in the afternoon in Harrods.

Nothing was what she had imagined. In the penthouse there were undercurrents, rifts, unhappiness. What she had counted on to be her safe London home, shared with a bliss-fully happy sister and brother-in-law delighting in their small son, turned out to be a shifting quicksand of tension and resentment.

After dinner they drank strong black coffee ('One thing I must admit about Anna, she does make good coffee. But then all Italians do,' Melissa commented) on the patio in the dusk while the evening breeze washed coolly over them, and the lights of the city pricked out into brilliance as the last of the sunset faded. Andrew poured brandy, and Emily knew that her London life had not only begun, but that like any life anywhere it was loaded with problems.

The first of these was already under discussion. Lunch on Sunday. Melissa proposed having it with Andrew at the

Hilton. Joan's day off, true, but Emily could stay at home to look after Barnaby, couldn't she?

Andrew vetoed the plan without hesitation, suggesting that they had a picnic on Hampstead Heath. Barnaby, he pointed out, would enjoy that. Melissa sighed, but Andrew had his way, and the next morning they all drove out to Hampstead in the big Mercedes. Long-skirted again, Melissa sat grumbling in front with Andrew, while Emily, in an old cotton frock she despised, attempted to cope with an excited and boisterous Barnaby in the back.

Although crowds thronged the heath on this sunny autumn Sunday, Hampstead, Emily saw at once, was still countryfied – and certainly much more easy-going than Knightsbridge.

'Yes,' she said. 'I see why you wanted to bring Barnaby here.'

'Melissa and I did discuss leaving the penthouse, at one time, and finding a house here with a garden for Barnaby to run about in.'

'Yes, yes. A godden for Bonby.'

'Barnaby.'

'I said. A godden for Baa-Baa-Baa-Baanby. So vere.'

'But Melissa was against it.'

'Oh well, Hampstead is all right on a day like this, I give you that. But it's hopelessly dead in winter. Taxis loathe coming out here, too. It's not practical.'

Andrew tweaked a pink curl. 'Much you know about practicality, my girl.' But he said it affectionately, and looked at Melissa with a naked sexual desire the equal of Greg's.

Melissa took instant advantage. 'Now a flat at the sea I wouldn't mind,' she suggested. 'Or abroad, even. A second home, in the sun. I think I'd rather care for that.'

'When I get shot of this Trinidad trip we'll think about it,' Andrew promised.

Melissa nodded. 'Let's do that.'

From that moment on she talked of nothing else, and when she went off with Andrew that evening, to drive the

Mercedes back to Knightsbridge from London Airport, she was canvassing the advantages of the riviera against the mountains. 'Or of course,' Emily heard her say in the hall as they were leaving, 'There are the Italian lakes, too.'

3. Central London Hospital

The day Emily began work at the Central coincided with the visit of two American VIPs to the cardio-thoracic unit. Northiam arrived in the theatre early that morning, flanked by the Americans, who had flown in from California around midnight. The surgeon, Professor Cohen, was small, rotund and bouncing – at home in his own hospital he was known as the india-rubber man, a reference not only to his walk but also to his resilience. He was accompanied by the medical specialist from his team, Dr Flanagan. He looked morose, a long streak of misery who, Sister asserted afterwards, spoke only three times during the six hours he spent in her theatre. What was evident to everyone, though, with or without speech, was the overwhelming respect these two Americans, highly respected in the heart field themselves, had for Northiam.

' 'Morning, Sister. Like to introduce our visitors. Professor Cohen, Dr Flanagan, from the cardio-thoracic department of the Ocean Hospital. You'll have read their book. They've crossed the Atlantic to be with us today – so I hope we're going to have something interesting to show them. Eh?'

Sycophantic murmurs all round, though not a soul in the room was unaware that this piece of surgery was going to be something of a Northiam *tour-de-force*. He had combed the recent admissions for a classic case to demonstrate to the Americans, who had written to him saying how much they admired his work, and that they had been particularly impressed by various details of his technique written up in the journals recently. Could they call in on their way to a symposium they were attending in Germany in the autumn? So here they were.

Northiam was introducing James Leyburn and Mark Corrie – on tenterhooks, and pasty-faced from an almost sleepless night coupled with nervous indigestion – his own medical specialist, Dr Amyas Miller, and the anaesthetist with his registrar. A small symposium then followed, as all of them began discussing not only the operation ahead, how Northiam intended to approach it, where their techniques were likely to differ, and why, but also the apparatus here in the Central and its equivalents in the Ocean Hospital.

The first incision was far behind them, the operation well under way, though downstairs in the unit office the day was just beginning, when Emily, in her beige trouser suit, newly washed, and her highest platform soles to give her much needed height, made her way along the corridors.

Wendy Stourbridge, who was Northiam's personal secretary and in charge of the office, heard Emily come clattering along the corridor like a herd of young ponies, and her heart sank.

Unsteadily, Emily stomped in, knees trembling in any case now that the moment of commitment was upon her, and the platform soles proving alarmingly unmanageable on polished floors.

Wendy greeted her encouragingly while her mind raced. What an infant she'd landed herself with – and those shoes were an added problem. Could she anchor the child to her desk today, so that Northiam – who, thank the lord, would with luck be more interested in his Americans than in new staff – might fail to spot his pet abomination of platform soles on the feet of her latest recruit to his office? At least he no longer objected to females in trousers. Since he'd married Felicity Esher a few years back his notions of feminine wear had been miraculously updated. If only Felicity would take to wearing platform soles, Wendy reflected, the question of staffing would be immensely simplified.

'I'm sorry your desk is a bit small,' she said. 'You'll be rather cramped to begin with, I'm afraid, but it's the best we can do at present. Sara is leaving in a few months – her husband's taking up a post in Glasgow – and then you can have hers.'

Tall and angular, with dark curls, and wearing the inevitable denim and cheesecloth, Sara grinned amiably, spoke ominously. 'Hi. Welcome to the chain gang.'

Wendy chose to ignore this, said only that Sara would show Emily where everything was kept. 'Meantime I'll clear any urgent problems out of the way and then I'll give you an idea of our daily routine – though in fact we tend to lead a hand-to-mouth existence here. The surgeons come in when they can, and we build the work around that. This morning they're all in the theatre, so it should give us a chance to catch up.'

'Much needed,' Sara added, apparently having appointed herself as some sort of Greek chorus signalling trouble. She showed Emily the stationery stocks, where the clean tapes were kept, and what seemed an unlimited collection of registers. System was all-important in Northiam's office, and everything had to be entered and recorded in a library of ledgers and notebooks 'if you so much as move it from one side of the desk to the other,' Sara said sardonically. 'And if you value your life you'd better not forget. Or Mr Northiam will have your guts for garters. If you ask me, he ought to be muzzled and led about on a lead, only let loose in the theatre to do his life-saving act – and there they need armour-plating. What James Leyburn goes through would finish any other man.'

'You exaggerate, Sara. As usual,' Wendy was crisp. A doctor's wife in her middle forties, whose children were at university, she was slim and tailored, with greying curls and a humorous expression. 'But I can't deny Mr Northiam is a difficult man sometimes. He keeps us all on our toes. As a surgeon he's outstanding of course. No doubt about it, he's quite the most brilliant man in London in his own field, and entitled to a few funny little ways. Don't let Sara put you off.'

Far from putting her off, all this talk served only to convince Emily that to work for this prickly difficult surgeon whom no one seemed able to understand would be a privilege, and the entrancing prospect that she might prove to be the first secretary capable of handling this brilliant monster beckoned her enticingly.

However, she had little opportunity to dwell on this glorious future. Instead the morning sank without trace as she pounded up and down corridors. First Sara showed her round the department, and then the way to the thoracic theatres, the laboratories, the X-ray department, physiotherapy, intensive care, the wards, outpatients – Emily was thankful she had already gained some idea of the hospital's geography on Saturday, for without this she would have been totally bewildered and lost. After this she was shown every nook and cranny in the office itself, down to which paper to use for which letters, where to run off stencils, how to work the copier, how Northiam liked ECG recordings to be attached to case-papers, and how to compile one stencilled sheet from operating lists, ward rounds and outpatient sessions and distribute it round the department. Wendy, who thought she was beginning to look punch drunk, sent her to lunch early with Sara, who employed the break in giving Emily the lowdown on Northiam.

'Rather you than me,' she warned her. 'I've only stuck him this long because I knew Bill would be leaving, and I didn't want too many changes. And anyway Wendy is great to work for, and you can learn so much from her. And then there's our James, after all. Everyone fancies him. But Northiam treats him like dirt sometimes – oh, not specially him, I don't mean. Everyone. His trouble is he expects top performance from every individual on his staff every second of every day. You'd think he could make a few allowances occasionally, be a bit helpful now and again – try to behave like a human being for once in a while. He won't, though. He never has. You'll find out.' Pausing for breath, and to gulp some of her apple crumble, Sara had second thoughts. 'Oh dear,' she said guiltily. 'Your first day, and you haven't even met the old devil yet. I hope I haven't put you right off?'

Emily, spooning up raspberry yoghurt, far from being put off, was only confirmed in her determination to succeed where others had failed, to be the one person recognised to be able to handle the great man in any of his moods. All that remained was to meet him.

No sign of him that afternoon. Instead, late on, a call from James, apparently in intensive care. He reported that Northiam, accompanied by the two Americans, had left for a late lunch with Felicity in the laboratory. After this, he told Wendy with suppressed laughter, Northiam and Felicity were taking off for Hampton Court with the Yanks.

'Hampton Court?'

'That's what the man said.'

'But – but – what about – ? There's an enormous pile of stuff here for him to sign, and a load of queries. I told everyone he'd be in this afternoon, and – '

James's chuckle floated clearly along the line. 'Not the first time, after all,' he said. 'You'll have to make his excuses. And I'll come in and do what I can as soon as I get through this lot here.'

'Thanks,' Wendy said. 'I'll expect you then.'

Half an hour later James appeared, with Mark Corrie.

'We got through more quickly than I expected,' he said. 'Hi, Emily. How are you doing?'

Emily had hardly the faintest idea, but in any case Wendy answered for her. 'She's doing very well,' she said quickly, anxious to grab James's attention for office problems. 'Now, we've sorted out the letters that you can sign for Mr Northiam, so would you mind doing them first, and then Emily can take them along to the post.'

'Right.' Sitting down at Wendy's desk, James began working his way solidly through the heap of letters and case-papers.

Sara came over to him with an additional pile. 'These are the ones I've done for you to sign yourself,' she said. 'Will you have them here with the others?'

'Sure.'

Now James was surrounded by a mountainous sea of paper. Emily, who'd been told by Wendy to remove the letters from the case-papers as he signed them, began packing them into their envelopes, making sure that the carbons went with the case-papers, and the X-rays in a separate pile, hovered at his shoulder, toppling on her platform soles. Her own desk in the corner had been appropriated by Mark Corrie, who seemed to be exchanging a separate series of letters, notes and tapes with Sara, while Wendy was conducting an impassioned dialogue on the telephone about an appointment that had to be changed.

All I have to do is keep my head, Emily told herself urgently. Don't panic. At all costs I must see that I don't make any sort of muddle. Better to be slow and keep things in order. She removed the letter James had just signed, put the carbon with the case-papers and the original in its envelope, and wondered how she meant to go on putting letters into envelopes like this, enter them in the essential little book, and make a pile of case-papers and another of X-rays as well, all without access to her own desk. Somehow she managed, and the pile in front of James grew smaller, while the three piles round Emily – one on a chair, two on the floor – grew larger, until they finished almost neck and neck.

He leant back, stretching wearily, but Emily was too busy counting to notice how tired he was. She was counting her envelopes, then her entries in the little book, then the case-papers. To her unutterable relief, the numbers matched.

'Right,' James was saying to Wendy. 'We've cleared the decks here. Any more for the *Skylark*?'

'There are rather a lot of queries that really ought to be dealt with today,' Wendy said apologetically. 'Suppose Emily takes that collection off to the post, I can do the queries with you.'

'Fine.'

'Hold on a minute, though, Emily. Have either of you had any sort of meal?'

Both men laughed hollowly.

'Breakfast, she must mean,' James said to Mark.

'And then we had a cuppa, didn't we? I can't remember exactly when. After the list. But no one invited us slaves to the spread in the lab.'

'I'm sure Emily wouldn't mind calling in at the canteen on her way back from the post.'

'Of course I will.'

'Smoked-salmon sandwiches all round, and champagne,' Mark suggested, with a broad grin.

'Surely that's not what Felicity is providing?' Wendy was shaken. 'Who are these Americans, anyway?'

'Professor Cohen and Dr Flanagan. And they sure are getting the treatment. I took the message myself. "Would smoked salmon be all right, and the wine was on ice, but ought she to send out for gin for the American, instead?" '

A deep sigh went round the office.

'And what did the great man have to say to that?' Sara enquired.

'His usual grunt. Which I duly translated for Madam into "perfectly splendid, and perhaps she'd better be on the safe side and send out for the gin". So she said that was what she thought, and she'd already done so.' He produced his chubby grin again, and surveyed them all benevolently. Corpulent already – he was under thirty – and ebullient, Mark Corrie, who looked like a jolly Dickensian grocer, was the possessor of a pair of hands whose surgical dexterity showed signs of rivalling James's own within another five years. 'Stewed tea and stale cheese sandwiches for us, and like it,' he added.

'I'll go with Emily, shall I, and help her carry – '

'Oh no, Sara love, you can't,' Mark interrupted. 'She'll have to manage. I want to give you this stuff before they bleep me.'

Emily's heart sank, and she hoped she'd be able to find the way. 'I shall be OK,' she said sturdily. After all, any moron ought to be able to fetch a tray of tea and sandwiches and take a few letters to the post.

'Bring a pot of tea, not cups,' Sara instructed her hastily. 'If you ask for a pot, they'll make it specially, and it'll be fresh.'

'But the main thing is to hurry,' Mark said.

'Here, take this.' James handed over a pile of loose change from his pocket.

Emily clattered out. Her feet were killing her. All day long she seemed to have been charging up and down corridors and staircases, in search of missing documents, elusive X-rays, case-papers, lab reports. Alternatively she had been dashing about delivering these same pieces of paper to someone who needed them and should have had them an hour ago – and usually said so. And now, as soon as the door shut behind her, she was in a tumult of anxiety. First, she might miss the post, and she knew at least half the letters carried details of appointments or admissions in the next day or two. Secondly, she might lose her way to the canteen, find a queue when she at last arrived, and then, when she returned to the office hours later, James would have gone. No tea. No sandwiches. Nothing since breakfast.

This was a hospital, she reminded herself. While she squawked away inside her head like a wet hen, around her people in pain were facing death with fortitude, or people like James and Mark were fighting to bring them back from death to a life worth living. To all of them, patients and doctors, a meal here and there was of no account. No one would particularly notice if she failed to deliver the goods. She'd better try to acquire a sense of proportion.

There was a queue. Of fat slobs who obviously got themselves outside three square meals a day and half a dozen snacks, too. She hated them. At last, panting, she clattered back along the corridors, and her relief at finding James and Mark still on station was as great as if, unaided, she'd delivered a baby in an ambulance or done an emergency tracheotomy with a penknife in mid-Atlantic.

They welcomed her with glad cries and fell on the food like hungry hounds. Through a full mouth, Mark remarked, 'Just as well his lordship's safely *en route* for Hampton Court. He wouldn't appreciate seeing the office turned into a snack bar.'

'Sometimes I wonder how he supposes his staff maintain life,' Wendy remarked dispassionately.

'He imagines we live on air. Simple. I've often noticed it.'

'Certainly, as long as I've worked for him we've had a running battle about snacks in the office. He will not grasp that frequently they're essential.'

James poured more tea. 'Well,' he said peaceably, 'there's something to be said for his side of the argument. With all

47

these VIPs dropping in from overseas, not to mention the lords and sirs calling in to chat about their patients at any odd hour, it mightn't look too good if the place was littered with dirty plates and yoghurt cartons, as they say the orthopaedic department is.'

'But think of the well-fed orthopods and their extra energy, initiative and brain-power. Our trouble is that there's nothing the great man enjoys more than living by rule. He thinks if he once gives permission for a ham sandwich in here, the place will instantly turn into a soup kitchen for the entire hospital. He never trusts anyone's discretion. That's his problem. Ours, however, is to achieve an adequate standard of nutrition.' Mark beamed, and swallowed an entire sandwich, folded in half, at one gulp.

'Is that the last tape, Mark?' Sara asked him. 'If so, do you mind if I clear off now? I promised to meet Bill at five-thirty.'

'No, that's my lot. Many thanks.'

'You go straight off,' Wendy told her. 'Emily and I can clear up here.'

'Thanks very much.' Sara was already kicking off the light flatties she'd been wearing all day, putting on sandals with platforms higher than Emily's.

So that was the secret. Emily made a mental note. She'd better write home for her gym shoes to wear around the hospital. Her running shorts, too, perhaps, and a stock of sweat shirts.

'If you're going to intensive care now, Mark,' James said, 'I'll come with you. We can look at today's cases first.'

'Right.' Mark rose. He and James went to the door.

'Thanks for the tea and sympathy,' James said pausing, his hand on the door handle. He looked across the room to Emily, who was squatting on the floor listing her pile of X-rays into a notebook. 'I'll be about an hour in intensive care,' he said. 'And then I must go to the ward. So I'll have a meal between eight and nine, I should think. Care to join me? Or will it be too late for you?'

Unaware of the small sensation he had produced in his other two hearers, Emily glanced up from the notebook,

48

pencil poised, one finger on the X-ray number, and assured him agreeably that after eight would be OK by her.

It was in fact eight-fifteen when he picked her up at Oriel House and, a little to her surprise, took her to a small but clearly expensive place in Soho, ordered wine and delicious food, almost, Emily thought, as if they had been celebrating.

'Well, so we are,' he said, when she pointed this out to him. 'Your first day at the Central.'

He meant this literally, he was slightly astonished to discover. The hospital was more home to him than his flat, and it had been extraordinarily satisfying to find Emily ensconced there in the office, part of his working family, and now to be able to end the day with her – this impossible day, when Northiam had been his most unpredictable, suddenly clearing off like that to Hampton Court. Offering him, too, a public snub in the theatre by failing to include him in the lunch invitation. Anyone else would have taken the entire team. Northiam never. But even he would normally include his first assistant, if no one else. To be able to sit quietly sharing a meal with this tranquil and engaging child was amazingly healing.

She'd changed, he saw, from the trouser suit, was wearing a long flowery skirt with some sort of clinging black top. She'd grown into a girl of great attraction, he realised. No doubt about it, she'd be in demand at the Central. This reflection failed to give him the pleasure he expected, and to prevent himself from analysing the reasons for the undoubted twinge of – of what? Surely not jealousy? No. Ridiculous – he began discussing a subject guaranteed to occupy his full attention at once, that morning's surgery and Northiam's odd behaviour.

Emily wanted nothing better than to listen to him recapping the day's surgery. 'Oh yes,' she said at once. 'How did it go in the theatre? What were the Americans like? Everyone was talking about them.'

'They were a very bright pair. Agreeable, too. And in fact the surgery went off like a dream. Northiam excelled himself. He was superb, and the Americans were visibly impressed. I daresay that's why he went off to Hampton Court

4

with them – though I suspect that was to take them out of my range, too. He wanted to let rip.' Of course that was it. Until he heard himself saying it, he hadn't grasped that this was the explanation for all Northiam's behaviour once the actual surgery had been completed.

'Let rip?' Emily was on to it at once. 'What about?'

'If I tell you, you must keep it to yourself. Not a word around the unit.'

'Cross my heart. And I'm quite reliable. I've been keeping secrets for ever – since I started helping out in the surgery years ago, when Dad swore me to silence with a sort of mini-Hippocratic oath. I don't even tell Melissa anything medical, ever.' Perhaps that was the wrong thing to say, though.

Apparently not. 'I should hope not,' he said shocked. 'Well, here goes.' He had to get it out of his system, or bust. 'And remember, not a word to anyone. Northiam and I have a longstanding difference about whether it's permissible to run down the health service to overseas visitors. He says it is. According to him, medicine is international, and this means we all share our failures and disasters as well as our triumphs. That's how we learn from one another's mistakes, and in the long term everyone benefits.'

'But you don't think so?'

'I'm not rational about it, as he's often pointed out. I hate it.' His voice grated. 'No matter how much he justifies it logically – and his reasons are perfectly sound, don't think they aren't. Absolutely valid – but to me it's unforgivable. In the theatre for instance, today, he was beginning to grumble to the Americans – admittedly he's been carrying on about it non-stop for weeks – about his great pacemaker scandal.'

'Sara said something about that at lunch, but – '

'You know what a pacemaker is, I suppose?' Unlike Melissa, who would have assumed a pacemaker to be a new trend in fashion, Emily probably did, he thought.

He was right. 'The little gadget that you implant to make the heart beat regularly,' she said precisely. 'When the bit of it that should be doing the job, the thing with the funny name, the – um – '

'The Bundle of His.'

'Has failed, or is unreliable.'

'Why didn't you do medicine?'

'Me?' She was startled. 'Why ever should I? My mother is a secretary, remember? And I'm like her, I enjoy office work, however incredible that may be to you. Just as you enjoy surgery. I like knowing what medicine is all about, but I couldn't practise it, like you and Dad. Go on about the pacemakers.'

'Well, inserting them is one of our regular bits of surgery. Both Northiam and I do a lot of it, and these days it's very safe – except, of course, that some of the patients we do it on are in a bad way before they reach us. But the procedure itself is straightforward enough – though, mind you, when your father was a student they wouldn't have been able to do it at all. No open-heart surgery in his day. It's all comparatively new. Life-saving, too.'

'So what's the row about?'

'The cost.'

'But if it's life-saving? Are pacemakers so dreadfully expensive, then?'

'Almost everything in heart surgery costs a hell of a lot. But the trouble here is that the pacemaker routinely used in the health service costs half as much as the one Northiam claimed the right to use when in his judgement it was required. And that's what the great pacemaker scandal at the Central is all about.'

'Is the one he wants to use so much better, then?'

'He doesn't want to use it all the time. Only in certain cases.'

'But it is much better for these particular cases?'

'To be fair, until recently no one – and that includes Northiam himself – was sure about this. But in the Central we've done a series of controlled trials, to find out, and the answer we've come up with is that there are occasions when it's desirable to use this more expensive version. Sometimes it may even prevent the patient needing a second operation at a later date – though there are other patients who are going to need surgery more than once in any case.'

'Does the expensive one cost so much more?'

'Ah well, this is what irritates Northiam so much. It only costs more in the eyes of a supplies officer, whose job is to purchase equipment, and who can't apparently see past the end of his nose. To an accountant costing the amount needed to run the department of cardiac surgery, the so-called cheap version – if it were to be used for these particular cases – would actually work out more expensive, because if it needed to be replaced you'd incur the full running costs of the theatre and the surgical team. So you'd end up spending a good deal more than the difference in cost between the two pacemakers, even if you only look at the problem from the financial angle. So Northiam – who in addition to being the senior heart surgeon at the Central, happens also to be the official adviser to the Department of Health – has produced a memorandum for the department, setting all this out, and listing, as well, the worth-while work surgeons could undertake in the time gained.'

'So he's proved any extra expenditure on each pacemaker is more than justified?'

'That's right. All over the bar the shouting, in fact. If only he'd shut up it would all sort itself out nicely now. What I object to is that at this stage he goes off and blows his top to these visiting Americans. All bureaucracies are slow, let's admit it, and I know only too well the health service can be appallingly long-winded. But the whole problem has been settled in principle, he only has to sit tight and wait, and it'll all be handed to him on a plate. Given the bare minimum of goodwill, this final flare-up could have been avoided.' He laughed shortly. 'No such luck. For months now, Northiam and the administration have gone out of their way to irritate and antagonise one another.'

'But surely the administrators realise who they're dealing with? I mean, Northiam's an international figure, he's famous all over the world for his surgery, a sort of celebrity. No administrator would dream of trying to interfere in what Northiam does in his own theatre, would he?'

'That, duckie, is exactly what someone has done.'

Emily stared. 'But how could they? Anyway, I thought

you said he was the Advisor to the Department of Health, so surely he only has to say what he thinks should be used?'

'In theory, yes. And in fact the department has already accepted his recommendations. But, of course, this decision had to weave its way through a series of committees before it could be sent out as official policy. It sometimes takes months, I'm afraid before new instructions percolate through to the place where the work is actually done. Even so, a directive about pacemakers has gone out from the department, and most hospitals have been acting on it for months. Just our luck, though, that our copy managed to lose itself in someone's pending tray, and in the meantime some thick-headed junior in the office took it on himself to inform our Mr Northiam that he was using the wrong pacemaker, and he should desist forthwith.'

'Someone in the office told Northiam he was using the wrong pacemaker?' Emily's voice rose incredulously.

'Em, my love, you're clearly a girl after Northiam's heart, and I prophesy a brilliant future for you in the Central. He'd go for that horrified tone of yours in a big way. At any rate, you understand now why he's so furious. He says the administration is trying to interfere in his clinical responsibility. He's reported the incident to everyone he can think of – the Royal College of Surgeons, the British Medical Association, and, of course, the Department of Health. I must admit, too, the health service would probably be better run if everyone reacted as strongly as he does to this sort of ham-handed behaviour. Anyway, there's been a most tremendous uproar, and today Northiam has obviously been itching to give the Yanks a blow-by-blow account of his war to the death with the administration. He kept making ironical references to 'independence of clinical judgement, which some of my more supine colleagues seem prepared to throw away' – that was a dig at me, you see – and promising to give the Americans the low-down on the takeover of the health service by faceless bureaucrats. And as he didn't invite me to join them for lunch, which normally he would do, and then cleared off to Hampton Court in that infuriating way, I guarantee that by now they've heard the full story.' He looked at his watch. 'Blast, I'll have to be off. I'm sorry, Emily, I'm as bad as Northiam, pinning you down all through your meal with my complaints about what goes on in the Central.'

'I've enjoyed every minute.'

'I'll put you in a taxi,' he said. 'I've let time run on, I'm afraid. Unless – ' He broke off. 'Have you been to intensive care yet? Did they show you round this morning?' He was oddly unwilling, he found, to part with her.

'They showed me round the department, and I saw the entrance to intensive care, so as to know how to find my way there. I haven't been inside.' She was hopeful. Would he take her with him? 'I would love to see the unit in action, if I could. Do you think – '

'You can come with me if you like. The only trouble is, it does mean you'll have to find your own way back.'

'That wouldn't matter at all,' Emily assured him fervently. 'I'll easily be able to get a taxi at the hospital.'

'All right then. We'll go along.'

4. London Days

In the Central it might have been midday instead of midnight. Bustle, greetings, a crowd – who all knew one another. Emily was the only outsider. This, though, didn't bother her. Accustomed since childhood to accompanying her father on his rounds and his visits to the local hospital, she remained glued to the air six inches behind James's shoulder, followed him into the lift, out into the entrance to intensive care.

Or perhaps foyer was more the word for this place where the atmosphere was somewhere between that of Melissa's favourite hotel, the Hilton, and a Swiss drug house. The quiet hush, the subdued efficiency, were unmistakably medical. Yet it carried more of the aura of private medicine, of a luxurious surgical nursing home – for Arab sheiks, perhaps – than of part of the familiar shabby old health service. Indeed, it often housed Arab sheiks, but anyone who needed its care could be admitted – anyone, that is, from the cardiothoracic unit, its wards, its theatres, its outpatients.

Electronic doors opened before them as they approached, lights flashed high up on walls, low down on metal consoles, there was a constant hiss and whirr of machinery, a great deal of polish and stainless steel, and – midnight or not – a throng of white coats and pastel stripes, a fair amount of only mildly subdued clatter and chat. A vast amount of apparatus, too. More than Emily had ever seen assembled in one place. Abandoned amongst it, the patients. Puny, frail, they seemed to be at the mercy of the machinery, though she knew it was this most of all which sustained their slipping hold on life.

The machinery and, of course, the staff. Neither could succeed without the other. People like James and Northiam.

And here suddenly, to her consternation, was Northiam himself. Not in the least what she'd expected, either. She'd imagined him to be a great bull of a man, overpowering and rowdy. But here he was, a tiny little figure with a cropped head, a small moustache, eyes like lasers. A small man with an alarming power output. Like a tidal wave, a formidable thrust of impatient authority met her, and she flinched involuntarily, longed to be able to disappear instantly, had a strong impulse, in fact, to turn round and rush headlong from the unit.

She succeeded in standing her ground, surviving James's brief introductions.

A second shock. Felicity Northiam. Could this slim and beautiful auburn-haired girl not only be a brilliant pathologist but married to this furious old man?

Others, of course, had experienced the same reaction before Emily. Twenty years younger than Northiam, Felicity had married him five years earlier, to the astonishment of her contemporaries at the Central.

For Felicity Esher, as she then was, had been the accepted girl friend of Tom Rennison in the days when he had been Northiam's first assistant. When Rennison had left the Central everyone had expected Felicity to follow him. But she had remained in her post at the hospital and in due course had married Marcus Northiam. It had been the sensation of the year.

Was she happy with him? Or did she remember Tom still? No one could say. Felicity's reserve was impenetrable.

There was no lack of prophets forecasting disaster. The only qualities Felicity and Northiam had in common, people said unkindly, were intellectual arrogance and impatience – an improbable basis for a happy marriage. In small ways, though, as they all agreed in the cardio-thoracic unit, she had changed Northiam for the better. He was beginning, for instance, to understand a little about fashion, and he'd even been known, occasionally – like once or twice a year – to accept the necessity for individuals on his staff to leave punctually for a hair appointment or to catch the butcher before he closed.

Emily, of course, knew nothing of this, thought only, once she'd recovered from the impact of Northiam, how young and beautiful Felicity was. Tall and slight, her red-gold hair caught in the nape of her neck, the pleated emerald chiffon she'd worn for dinner with the Americans at the Waldorf, where they were staying, swirling round her ankles, Felicity was riveting.

What Emily never suspected was the impact she made. The eyes of the cross old man and the beautiful redhead met, momentarily, in startled marital interrogation. As soon as they were alone together, 'Has James found himself a girl at last, do you suppose?' Northiam asked.

'Not only found one, but imported her into the office, apparently.'

'This bears watching.'

And so the rumour that had been born when James invited Emily to dinner with him that night spread like a forest fire.

That evening, though, Northiam behaved as if she were invisible, saying only, in his curt, incisive tones, immediately after the introductions, 'I came in to look at this morning's case, James.'

'Of course.'

'I'll leave you to it,' Emily said hastily to the air between herself and the departing backs. Down in the busy lift, out into the courtyard, between the high buildings, and through into the quiet square.

Well after midnight now, and instead of returning to Knightsbridge in a taxi, as James supposed, she walked on, thinking about the day behind her, knowing herself at last part of this great teaching hospital, working for its surgeons, treading its corridors – never again on platform soles, though – in her own right. And, final triumph, crowning point of a first day that had more than lived up to her expectations, she'd just left the intensive-care unit, where she'd met her chief, the internationally celebrated Marcus Northiam. This was London life, and it was her scene for sure.

On the far side of the square, as she approached, she could

see light coming from the basement of the house with the peacock door. She walked on, hesitated momentarily by the area steps. Melissa would be there, with Greg.

Her sister had been noticeably put out, in fact, to hear that Emily was going out with James. 'Oh, you don't want to spend the evening with *him*,' she'd expostulated. 'Can't you get out of it somehow? It'll only be a fearful drag, and I want you to come over to Greg's place with me. I told him we'd both be coming.'

'I promised James.' Emily had been firm, and she'd stuck it out when Melissa made a bit of a fuss. 'If you'd only warned me I could have told him I wasn't free. But I can't back out now.'

'Try and get away from him early, anyway, and then come on over,' Melissa had said.

Nearly one in the morning was hardly early, but very likely Melissa would still be there. The sound of a guitar floated up to her, and in spite of her fatigue, the throbbing music and the voices drew her, and she went down the steps and into the flickering candlelight, so mysterious and inviting, offering laughter and romance and an intangible excitement.

That first day was to set the pattern for them all. Every one was packed, five hours' sleep became her average. At seven each morning she fell blindly out of bed, woke herself up under the shower, breakfasted in the nursery with Joan and Barnaby – Melissa seldom woke before ten – and left to join the rush-hour crowds at the Tube station.

From that moment on she was surrounded by people – at the Central throughout the working day, and on into the evening too. In the office she succeeded in keeping her head, registering each detail in one of the little books. She was accurate and methodical, and her shorthand was excellent, so that Wendy was soon finding her far more reliable than the slapdash Sara. What handicapped Emily was her typing, much slower than Sara's, though steadily improving, as – to her unbounded relief – was her recognition of the varying individuals who came in and out – physicians, pathologists

(Wendy's husband one of them), radiologists, respiratory physiologists (Sara's husband), biochemists, anaesthetists. The list went on endlessly, and at first she'd been highly embarrassed if she failed to place them when they telephoned or called in. She grew hot for weeks afterwards whenever she recollected one of her early gaffes. She mistook Dr Amyas Miller, the eminent and brilliant medical specialist in Northiam's team, for Fred, the relief porter. As it was a fact, though seldom mentioned, that these two men did indeed look and sound alike (to put it bluntly, both of them were fat cockneys), everyone fell about laughing as the tale of Emily's howler swept round the unit. 'Not to brood, love,' Sara said cheerfully. 'We all go through it.'

Northiam himself Emily continued to find terrifying. However, they assured her on all sides that he obviously had a soft spot for her, and that this in itself ensured her a future in the department.

Within a week or two, she was surrounded by hopeful young men eager to take her out. Mark Corrie, for one, and a number of house physicians and surgeons she encountered on her rounds. One of the administrators, too wanted to date her, as well as Matthew, the lanky, drawling Australian with the straw-coloured hair who, for all practical purposes, lived in his shabby Dormobile in St Anne's Square. Matthew's bird was waiting for him at home, or so he hoped. He showed Emily photographs of his parents' house outside Sydney, and this girl, Jackie, he was going to marry when he'd completed his postgraduate thesis and returned down under. He took Emily sightseeing in the creaking Dormobile, working his way methodically through his guide book, chugging out – like Northiam and the Americans, except that they'd gone in Northiam's Rolls – to Hampton Court, or to Windsor Castle, Canterbury Cathedral, Oxford and Cambridge. When she went with him Emily shared expenses, paid for half the petrol, and they ate cheaply, brewing up in the van – a very different set-up from an evening in the penthouse.

In fact, she soon found she was living in three separate worlds. The hospital, the two houses in St Anne's Square with the peacock doors, and Knightsbridge. The three didn't mix, and she learnt not to try to interpret the Central to Greg or Melissa, nor what he insisted on referring to as 'your drop-out friends at the end of the square' to James.

James stood out head and shoulders above the rest of them, and for her the essence of the Central was to be found in a passing glimpse of him as he went between theatre, intensive care, wards and outpatients. Bulky, kindly, plain and slow-spoken, he radiated reassurance and integrity.

He had appointed himself, there could be no doubt of it, her guardian and protector, keeping a fatherly eye on her from day to day. That first evening, when he'd taken her out to a meal, was followed by other invitations – once a week, regularly, he'd ask her to join him at the end of the day.

In the office the telephone would ring, and she'd pick it up. 'Em? James here.'

Not that that necessarily meant anything, of course. Often his next words would be 'Is that tape ready yet? I want to . . . ' Or it might be 'Are those letters done?'

With luck she'd be able to say : 'I'm on the last one now.'

'Great. As soon as you've done it, could you rush them over to me in outpatients? If you can get them here within the next ten minutes I'll sign them before I go up to the wards, and you can get them off.'

But sometimes he'd say : 'Em? Care for a meal tonight? I was thinking perhaps we might . . . '

Often, of course, she had to say no. She'd already promised Matthew to go to a museum, perhaps, or Mark Corrie, who enjoyed exploring little restaurants listed in the *Good Food Guide*, would have booked her to sample one with him. She couldn't, after all, keep every evening free on the off-chance that James might ring.

When she did join him, in any case, he often behaved as if he were still in outpatients assessing the regime of one of his dimmer and more youthful post-operative patients. Emily scoffed openly at his cross-examination about her movements and diet, teasing him about his attitude to her with the casual cheek of the younger sister she felt herself to be. But though she didn't admit it even to herself, she liked the sense of security his interest brought her, and most of all she enjoyed his company. For James was nice to be with. Soon she began to look forward to her evenings with him, dressed carefully for them in order not to let him down. He was, after all, so very senior.

When a group from the unit went out for a celebration, she was accepted as his usual partner. Once or twice the party even included Northiam and Felicity, and finally an evening came when she was invited to partner James to a dinner the Northiams gave to a distinguished surgeon and his wife from Cairo. On this occasion Emily cadged a dream of a frock off Melissa. Her sister, a head taller than Emily, lent her a calf-length dress which, when Emily wore it, swept the floor, a misleadingly simple drift of tangerine pleating which set off her dark beauty to perfection, and did something quite extraordinarily disturbing as far as her figure was concerned, so that even Northiam gave her a glance noticeably different from his usual suspicious glare.

'What a heavenly dress, Emily,' Felicity said at once. 'Not Yuki, by any chance?'

'Yes, it is. It's my sister's actually – I didn't want to let you all down in this place.' She threw a slightly harassed eye round the Dorchester.

James promptly hugged her. 'As if you could,' he exploded, left his arm reassuringly round her shoulders, while Northiam and Felicity exchanged knowing looks.

On other evenings, though, they didn't dress up at all. James took her tramping through the London streets – sometimes eastwards, through the deserted City of London itself, financial and commercial centre of the capital, showing her not only Wren's masterpiece, St Paul's, but the smaller City churches he'd rebuilt after the Great Fire of 1666. Older churches too, whose names reflected the business of the walled City as it had been centuries earlier. St Michael's, Cornhill, and St Mildred's, Bread Street, or St Catherine by the Tower, and St Andrew's by the Wardrobe. And, for contrast, a favourite of Emily's, St Nicholas Shambles.

Together, too, they explored the squares, the narrow alleys, the hidden corners and the secret gardens that flourished so unexpectedly between grimy buildings and roaring traffic. Late roses bloomed under St Paul's, and there were roses, too, in the garden of St Sepulchre Without Newgate, bombed out of existence during the London blitz in 1940. In Russell Square, surrounded by its outrageous architectural medley of styles – from the terracotta Gothic extravagance of the Russell Hotel on the east to the concrete and plate-glass chunks of the new Law School to the north – they floodlit their roses at night. London, it seemed to Emily, walking through the squares with James, was a city of flowers and tall trees.

For years, ever since he'd first come to the Central as a student, James had walked the London streets. A cheap form of recreation, it had been, and then, too, he'd often been trying in those early days to work the misery and conflict out of his system, to clear his mind, as he told Emily one evening, when she'd been explaining how she squirmed daily when she thought what a fool she'd made of herself on the occasion when she'd confused Dr Amyas Miller with the porter.

James's immediate response to this, like Sara's, was to say, 'It happens to all of us, you know.'

She'd looked at him, big and burly in his expensive suiting, one of the leading figures in her world, and found it impossible to accept what he said.

Being Emily, she told him so.

They'd been strolling through Russell Square, one of James's regular haunts, with its lawns, tall trees and the three fountains in the centre. He'd put a brotherly arm round her shoulders, gave her a quick hug. 'I assure you,' he'd said 'a good deal worse than that. I used to squirm almost hourly, you know, in the early days. I've often walked round this very square reliving my catastrophic errors, dying the death.' He glanced quickly at her, caught her amazement, tinged with a degree of scepticism. 'Oh, it may have looked great to outsiders to see James Leyburn suddenly part of Northiam's top team in the cardio-thoracic unit – and certainly when my appointment came through I was over the moon – but to live it day by day, I can tell you, Em, that was no sort of triumph. Very much the opposite. After all,

I'm a slow, fairly steady-going sort of character, while Northiam is fast as they come, and very impatient with it. To be truthful, he used to give me hell. And I put up with it. I had to – I didn't know how to deal with it, except by leaving. And that I wasn't going to do, not at any price.' Often he had been tempted to explode, to tell the old bastard what he could do with himself and his flaming job, but he'd been determined to hold this post down, to continue to learn from this unbearable man who happened to be one of the most brilliant heart surgeons in the country. So he'd clenched his teeth and got on with the job. Afterwards, though, he'd paid for his self-control, and as he walked the London streets his emotions churned.

'Even when I became his registrar we'd be at odds half the time. For instance, I might be talking to a patient, going slowly because he was still in a state of panic, alarmed by all the paraphernalia of a high-powered unit – flashing lights, monitors, the lot. You know how it is. Then I'd suddenly feel Northiam champing away behind me, willing me to get a move on, cut short the somewhat diffuse explanations the patient was indulging in.' He'd had his own obstinacy, though, and he'd seldom given in to this pressure. He'd finished with the patient at his own speed, not Northiam's.

'Then, you see, Northiam would take it out of me later. There'd be cutting little phrases in front of the visitors and students on his ward round.'

Emily had heard the same tale from the chubby Mark Corrie, mocking himself from twinkling slit eyes already half hidden in folds of flesh. But James had lived through this too? An entirely new light on him, this shed, for until now she'd seen him as self-confident, his position in the Central assured and established. But on these magical evenings in the leafy London squares, among the late roses and the dahlias, the chrysanthemums and the Michaelmas daisies, under a darkening sky, she was coming to know a different James, not only more complicated but much more vulnerable than she'd ever imagined.

And as they walked the streets together, James found himself telling Emily what it had been like to be young, and poor, and uncertain. First a student, then a raw young house surgeon. And as he talked to her, the boy he'd thought left behind in the past seemed to have joined him again, to be walking alongside Emily with him, until they fused and became one, and he felt much younger and immensely more cheerful. Finally, as autumn slipped into winter, he found that just as he'd shared his past with Emily, now he wanted to share the future, and he faced the fact that what he wanted was for Emily to remain in his life. For ever. Why not, after all? There was nothing against it. He wasn't Methuselah.

But then the next day, it might be, coming hopefully into the office, ready to take her out, he'd find her laughing with Mark Corrie, see her go off for the evening with him. Or he'd pass her on St Anne's Square, talking earnestly to Matthew, getting into his Dormobile and driving away.

His new-found optimism ebbed. These were her contemporaries. In self-protection he decided to see less of her, but somehow never came round to putting this decision into effect. Indeed, if anything, they seemed to be spending more time together.

This particular Saturday morning Emily had met him at the Central after his ward round. They decided to walk down to the river, and set off briskly, across to Lincoln's Inn Fields, and past the buildings of the Royal College of Surgeons. 'I sat for my Fellowship there,' he told her. The portico was impressive, she thought, the building flanked on one side by the red brick of the Imperial Cancer Research Fund Laboratories and on the other by the Nuffield College of Surgical Sciences. A centre of the surgical establishment, she told herself, wondering what it had been like to be James, going in there, a young surgeon trying for a postgraduate qualification.

They went on down towards Fleet Street and finally reached the river and the Victoria Embankment. There was a watery sun, a strong wind blowing and, beyond the pale blue lamp-posts with their white dolphins, the slap of the tide running hard. Across the river, on the south bank, Emily could see the rectangular blocks, like gun emplacements, of the National Theatre, next to it, past the bridge, the Queen

Elizabeth Hall and the Royal Festival Hall, its architecture fatally influenced, so her father always maintained, by the Nissen huts of the war years.

'The Royal Festival Hall and the National Theatre,' she commented. 'Do you know, I've still not been inside either of them. Rather disgraceful, really.'

James had been staring at the masts, stark against the sky, of *Discovery*, the ship that had taken Scott to the Antarctic. There was a small Bermudan sloop, too, swinging about on a mooring – no more, he estimated, than about twenty-five feet in length overall. If he owned a boat like that, he thought, he and Em could sail London's river. He turned a startled gaze on her. 'Festival Hall?' he repeated vaguely. 'National Theatre? Oh well, if you're set on going, I suppose I could take you one evening.' He sounded like any husband of long-standing, resigned to the inevitable.

Emily turned a radiant face to him. 'Would you, James?'

'I'm not much of a theatre-goer, I'm afraid,' he informed her, sighing, seeing his middle-aged self, unvarnished. Exactly as Melissa always said, he was boring. Here he was, at the weekend, free of the Central for eight hours or so, a lovely bird by his side. And what was he planning? To sail a boat. It would be cold and wet and uncomfortable, yet if he possessed it he'd expect Emily to share his joy in it, just as he expected her to tramp round London with him, wearing out shoe leather and listening to tedious tales about his days as a medical student. Other people – Matthew, Mark Corrie for instance – took her to places like Greenwich or Knole, or fed her wonderful food in well-known restaurants. No doubt, too, they had more to discuss than surgery and the geography of London. 'I'm no good to you,' he announced furiously, out of the blue. 'I've never been much good at doing any of the usual things. You want a young man to take you about, not an old bore like me, only interested in cardiology and the back streets of London.' As a proposal of marriage the statement left a good deal to be desired.

Certainly Emily didn't recognise it as such. Turning eyes larger than ever with astonishment on him, she said only, 'But I love coming out with you. Otherwise I wouldn't do it.'

5

Even in his present mood James could see this for himself, but he found no encouragement in the remark. Melissa's memory intruded. Like her, Emily no doubt found him useful. Undemanding and safe, probably. That would be it. A relaxing change, no doubt, from all the young men who badgered her to leap into bed with them – well, naturally they would. He would himself if he hadn't decided – no. This was no good. Forget it. He sighed again. He was one of those hardworking, backbone of the hospital sort of people, he reminded himself, whom everyone relied on to see things through. That was his strength, if he had one. No charisma, though. And he didn't make up for his deficiencies by being immensely good company, like young Mark Corrie, for instance, that budding bon viveur and raconteur. He wasn't a man for discos, or ear-shattering pop blaring at him, either. After all, he couldn't afford to be deafened daily. He and Northiam, as much as Amyas Miller, the real wizard, could pick up heart sounds through the stethoscope that were diagnostic, but that few others, even in the Central, could catch. No, he wasn't the type for racketing about socially. No good thinking he was going to change either. He wasn't. That way led to disaster. He'd tried to do it for Melissa, and it had been a mistake. Their marriage, if it had ever taken place, would have been a failure. They were unsuited.

Even Emily, whom he was beginning to think he loved as much as life itself, would have to take him as he was, or leave him.

Well, she'd leave him, that was for sure.

Momentarily he longed, ridiculously, to be brilliant, sophisticated and handsome, as good looking as that silly boy Greg, say, so that Emily might fall wildly in love with him. 'I wish I wasn't such a second-rate nonentity,' he blurted out, and immediately, ashamed, longed to recall the words.

'Second-rate? Nonentity? You?' Emily turned her wide startled gaze on him for the second time in a few minutes. 'You can't think that. Everyone in the unit depends on you, you hold the place together. No one else. How long do you think Northiam could keep his staff, if you weren't there?'

Three months had taught Emily a great deal about Northiam and the cardio-thoracic unit. 'He may be a brilliant surgeon, but the credit for the unit's success belongs as much to you. Everyone says so. He wouldn't achieve any of his magnificent results if you hadn't welded everyone into a team for him. Who is it they all turn to when there's a problem, too? Northiam? Not likely. You, every time.'

James, without intending to do anything of the sort, put his arm around her. 'Em,' he said, 'I love you. You make me feel a man again.' Just in time, he diverted the kiss he seemed to be going to give her so that it landed innocuously on her cheek. Her slight young body was amazingly soft against his, and he wanted to go on standing like this, holding on to her, here in full view on the embankment.

Instead he set off fast. 'Come on,' he said curtly. 'We'll go across the bridge, book some seats in the theatre, and have lunch in the restaurant at the Festival Hall.'

As they walked over the footbridge together, James looked down at the river beneath, at a tug towing a string of barges, saw the sun glinting on the foam from its bow wave, and knew himself lost in love with this young, slight girl at his side, her face with its fine bones etched against the sky, her dark hair blowing in the wind.

In the restaurant they found a table overlooking the river, and scanned the north bank from which they'd come. Or Emily did.

James went on watching Emily. Under one of the flowery padded waistcoats that were all the rage that autumn, she wore an apricot silk polo-neck. All these soft yellows, oranges and pinks, he thought – he would have alleged he never knew what women wore – were the right colours for her, brought out her dark glowing beauty. As she talked to him, her shining hair fell across her cheek, while her wide mouth that he had so nearly kissed crinkled into the smile he loved.

The smile he loved, and the girl he loved. He had no more doubts.

She'd lost weight since she came to London, and her skin had a transparency now that made her eyes seem even larger and more liquid. Or was this, he asked himself, more a symptom of the state of his own feelings than any actual change in Emily? He only knew he found her lovely and infinitely desirable, longed above all to possess her for the rest of his days. But when he searched the soft brown eyes for an answering surge of passion he met only the clear candour of Melissa's younger sister, honest and unafraid.

Prosaically, he enquired which evening she'd like to go to the theatre.

'Well,' she said, fishing out her diary, 'I'll have to fit it in with my evenings at No. 5.'

'Of course,' he agreed, his heart plummeting into his well-polished shoes. He already knew that she spent several evenings a week helping out in the office there with Greg's delinquent children, and he couldn't prevent himself from seeing this as a rejection of what he had to offer, a turning towards her own age group and away from him. 'Of course,' he said again, sadly. He'd dreamt up a load of rubbish. The sooner he forgot it the better.

5. Greg

Emily's evenings in the office at No. 5 opened her eyes in more ways than one, and showed her sides of the life that went on in the two half-derelict houses with the peacock front doors that she would never have suspected. For instance, there was a tough hardworking group running the hostel at No. 5 – which normally housed between twenty and thirty children, for periods varying from two or three days to as much as six months. William, the stocky, bearded young warden, was a social worker, at the same time dedicated and realistic. His wife Susan, a luscious overweight blonde, was capable of mothering the most unbearable child – and the staff and students too. These two were the backbone of the outfit. Then there was a psychiatrist who gave two evenings a week, a young clergyman who did the same, and two secretaries who came from their daytime jobs, as Emily did, to shift the untidy mess of paperwork that accumulated to toppling piles in the little office. Carmel and her friend Ruby prepared high tea almost every day before going on night duty at the hospital, and several housewives came in while their own children were at school, to clean, wash, mend or cook. And then there were the students. Some of them worked until they were ready to drop, anything from cleaning, repairing, painting, putting up shelves, to teaching, giving individual tuition or carrying out intensive casework. But there were others who were there only because they had latched on to a useful racket, their main occupation being to lounge around, talking and gossiping and drinking Nescafé – and making sure of a free bed in the big first-floor dormitory. The availability of these beds was Greg's achievement – as was the whole take-over of No. 4, inaugurated originally to put some voluntary helpers up overnight if they had transport problems after working late. Nowadays, though, the dormitory was more or less monopolised by a crowd of student layabouts.

One fact remained paramount. The houses behind the peacock front doors throbbed with vitality. However tired she was at the end of a hard day at the Central, the moment Emily entered the untidy office off the hall, where the telephone rang almost as often as it did in the cardio-thoracic unit, her energy and zest were magically renewed.

Her job, apart from clearing the typing and filing, consisted mainly of taking down and relaying long involved messages from parents, teachers or social workers – or, when the worst had happened, a far from infrequent occurrence, from police or probation officers. Greg spent his days escorting delinquent or absconding children, interviewing parents, foster parents, teachers, social workers, youth club leaders, and meeting trains that might or might not prove to carry missing limbs of Satan. None of this seemed to Emily to have much to do with teaching, though Greg had a double first from Cambridge. Melissa had told her proudly one evening when she was hanging about in the office waiting for him to return, loudly deploring his hopeless sense of time, while criticising Emily's clothes as a sideline – 'Must you always wear that dreary old denim?'

Emily made friends through the office at No. 5. To be honest, although they were the ostensible reason for her own presence and that of everyone else, she liked the children least. They seemed a poor lot, either out of hand or furtive and untrustworthy, though she told herself her attitude only demonstrated her own lack of any vocation for helping them. Sick people, yes. Any day. Thieving, malicious, filthy-tongued children – no.

Carmel agreed with her. 'Someone should take a stick to most of them, it's the only way,' she said. 'Greg's far too soft.' She smiled broadly, showing pearly white teeth, and shook the dark hair she had straightened as regularly as Melissa had hers curled. 'But then he's right soppy, isn't he?

You'd never find me standing for that language they hand out to him. They only laugh behind his back, too, so what's the use? You know what they call him?'

It turned out to be 'The Golden Wonder'. The nickname held an undercurrent of contempt that jolted Emily. For these children Greg was prepared to go without meals, tramp London for hours each day, even neglect Melissa – yet their response was to abuse him to his face and behind his back treat him as no more than a joke.

By now the first shattering impact Greg made on her had worn off. He was beautiful but, she had to admit, a little dull and more than a little weak. Kind, though, and well meaning – and, always, the spirit behind the haphazard, disorganised but joyous evenings in the basement kitchen where he and Melissa lived out their love. Somewhere between eight and nine, Greg would leave William and Susan to be responsible for the children, and retreat to his basement next door with Melissa, where they'd be joined by any of the students or voluntary helpers who cared to come.

By ten at night, a meal of some sort would be contrived from whatever oddments they were able to drum up between them. Sometimes they'd have a fry-up, at others a salad, from Scotch eggs, coleslaw, cottage cheese. Baked beans were a regular standby, and there'd be tins of coke and Nescafé. Occasionally someone in funds would bring in a barbecued chicken and a litre of wine, one of the students would strum a guitar, and they'd have a party, singing until the small hours, occasionally smoking pot. Emily and Melissa might go home to Knightsbridge in a taxi or Matthew would drive them in his old Dormobile. Often, though, Melissa remained in the basement with Greg, while Emily borrowed the old sleeping bag from the cupboard in No. 5 and spent the night in Carmel's bedroom, dropping into the sleep of exhaustion as soon as her head touched the tatty old cushion that served her as a pillow. Carmel would rouse her when she came in the next morning, and Emily would have to dress hastily and tear across the square in order to reach her office by nine o'clock, leaving a sleeping house behind her. She'd skip breakfast on these mornings, go hungry until the coffee break when, with luck, she'd have a chance to grab a cheese roll from the canteen.

The days were drawing in now, in the early mornings the air had a bite, and from Carmel's attic window, with the trees in the square standing stark and leafless, Emily could see across to the graceful terrace on the west side, pick out the tall windows of James's sitting room.

In Knightsbridge there were bonfires of fallen leaves in the squares, blue smoke rising in the still autumn air. In the penthouse the chairs and tables from the patio had been packed away for the winter, and the contractors who looked after the plants and shrubs had been to remove them.

At breakfast Barnaby was always asking Emily about the hospital. 'What's ve Central? Why you go evvy day? What *do*?' Emily produced a somewhat garbled version of a day at the Central London Hospital, unlikely to have been recognised by its consultants. 'What's typing? Show me typing? Why can't I – 'Anyway, why didn't she come home for tea? 'You could play wiv me in my barf.'

Emily explained about the office in St Anne's Square.

'I need you here,' he complained, looking and sounding distinctly elderly, a conventionally demanding man of the house, expecting his womenfolk round him, not gadding about all over London. 'And Mummy too,' his complaint ended.

'That's right. She helps as well.'

'Why not me, then? I want there too. Snan Skair.' He glared belligerently across his mug.

'St Anne's Square,' Emily repeated automatically, Melissa and Andrew having strong views on Barnaby's speech, determined he should learn words accurately from the beginning.

'Yes. I said. Snan Skair. You go. Why not me?'

Why not indeed, if he wanted to so much? Emily wondered if she could take him on Joan's next day off.

'I could bring Barnaby over, I thought. On Sunday afternoon, say. He's longing to come.'

'What a good idea,' Susan, who'd called in to collect Greg

for a discussion next door with one of the problem children, backed Emily at once.

Melissa brushed the suggestion aside impatiently. 'He's far too small to be dragged about all over London. Besides, one of us would have to lug him home at tea-time. Small children need their routine.'

'Much you know about routine, Melissa,' Matthew commented with a chuckle.

Melissa shot him a quelling glance, then relented and smiled instead.

'I'd take him back, too,' Emily insisted. 'He does so want to come over here. I could bring him on the bus – he'd love that.'

'I do think you ought to bring him over here.' Susan looked worried. 'After all, if you and Greg – oh well, another time. Come on, Greg, William's waiting, and he's got Jo with him.'

They both left, and Matthew soon departed also, saying he had letters home to write. As soon as the door shut behind him, Melissa turned to Emily. 'I'm sorry if I sounded cross, Em. But for goodness' sake shut up about bringing Barnaby here.'

'I just thought –'

'Well don't. Can't you see, he'd be bound to start talking at home about it, and about Greg, too. I'm not having that, thanks very much. So don't mention it again, will you?'

Others, however, were to keep the subject alive, and Melissa found herself under pressure. Susan even – in the office in the evenings – took to urging Emily to use her influence on her sister. 'We must all get together over this.' She was vehement. 'Otherwise it simply isn't fair to Greg or Barnaby. Melissa must let them get to know each other, and the sooner the better, it seems to me.'

William took a hand, too. 'Susan's quite right about this,' he assured Emily seriously, pinning her down in the hall as she came in one evening. 'Melissa ought to bring Barnaby over here with her as often as she can. After all, if Greg gets this job he's after, Melissa will go with him – that's the whole point of it – and they can't just drag Barnaby along with them with no preparation. He must have time to get used to Greg.'

Emily had heard all about the job Greg was hoping to land at an independent grammar school in the country, where he and Melissa would share a cottage, make their own bread, their own yoghurt, eat produce from their own garden. She didn't believe any of it.

The months in the penthouse had opened her eyes. Melissa, Emily felt sure, had no intention of leaving Andrew. At home in Knightsbridge, she continued to pore over brochures, amassing a selected pile for him to consider when he returned from Trinidad. She talked constantly about flats in Switzerland or the south of France, villas in Spain or Majorca. Nothing, though, was said about a cottage in Somerset with Greg. Finally Emily ceased to worry about Andrew and Barnaby. Instead she grew almost panicky on Greg's behalf. What was going to become of him? He was so terribly in love, and he was planning to alter his entire way of life for Melissa's sake, imagining she was ready to do the same. At last, one evening when she and Melissa were for once alone together in the living room of the penthouse, she nerved herself to tackle her outright.

'Everyone's talking about this job of Greg's. They seem to think you'll be leaving with him.' She stared accusingly at her sister. 'It's not true, is it?'

'Oh, Em, I know that's what they all think. But it's nothing to do with me, this wretched job he's found. I've begged him again and again not to leave London.'

'But he seems to think you'll go with him. And take Barnaby too.'

Melissa pushed her hands through her pink curls – paler, these days, and longer, too, framing her face. 'No good blaming me, Em. He doesn't listen to a word I say. All I want, and I keep telling him so, is for us to go quietly on as we are. Of course we can't see as much of each other as we'd like, but this way at least no one need be upset.'

Not much they needn't, Emily reflected grimly. She regarded her sister helplessly. Somewhere in the course of the past months, the awed admiration with which she'd viewed Melissa for as long as she could remember had changed, had become a quite different emotion, a tolerant and affectionate understanding shot across at increasingly frequent intervals with bouts of sheer exasperation.

She raised the problem of Melissa and Greg with Matthew one day when, exhausted and famished after one of his mammoth sightseeing tours, they were consuming a great bowl of corned-beef hash in his van. Matthew stirred his bowl thoughtfully, watched the steam rise. 'It's not really Melissa's fault, I don't think,' he surprised Emily by saying. 'She's only the excuse for a change that he wants to make anyway. After all, Greg's not exactly cut out for dealing with delinquents in a city centre, anyone can see that. He's far too academic – he'll be much more use with a group of seniors taking their A levels at grammar school, instead of mucking about the way he is now.'

'But –'

'He's lost with these young ruffians. They do as they like with him – he's afraid to challenge them, so he's everlastingly giving in, placating them. And they know it.'

'That's what Carmel says. But –'

'Everyone's spotted it. Except Greg himself, the poor sap. But if you ask me he's simply using your sister as an excuse, so that he can make his getaway without letting on – to himself or anyone else – that he's flopped.'

This had the ring of truth, and, indeed, came as no surprise to Emily, who had seen for herself over the months that behind his misleading good looks Greg was weak as water.

'Now, when I first came here,' Matthew was continuing, 'Greg used to sleep in No. 5 and share the supervision with William and Susan twenty-four hours a day. But then he started up these evening sessions in the basement in No. 4 – he said they gave the voluntary workers and the students a chance to let off steam and ask questions, with no kids around. But it wasn't that at all. My word, it wasn't. Oh no, it was to give old Greg himself a break, that's what. He conned the council into giving him a free hand in No. 4 – opened those big blue eyes of his at that silly old bag in the office, I reckon – and now he clears off around eight in the evening, and No. 5 doesn't see him again much before midday. And then he only looks in before making the rounds of the kids' families, teachers, social workers – you name it, Greg has a reason for interviewing them as long as they're not the kids themselves. It's all one big alibi, to keep him away from the children. Anyway, William and Susan will be glad to see the back of him. In his present frame of mind he's no more than a liability. That's why they're so keen to see him all fixed up with your sister – so that he'll clear off to his new job, and they can have a replacement who'll be some use.'

It was Carmel, though, who was the first to go. One evening she dropped into the office, bubbling with delight and pleasure. She'd achieved her ambition at last. She and Ruby had been allocated a flat in the big block on the other side of the square. 'The boys are coming to move my stuff on Saturday morning,' she told Emily, teeth flashing in a beaming, irrepressible smile.

Carmel had had her name down for this unfurnished flat for years, had been sleeping in the primitive attic at No. 4 and working in No. 5 each evening simply in order to save up for furniture. Tomorrow afternoon, she told Emily, she was going on a buying binge. 'So I won't be able to cook tea, I've told them. But of course, once I've moved, I'll go on helping them out until they find someone to take my place.'

That night, over supper in the basement at No. 4, a poor view was taken of Carmel's departure.

'Of course,' Greg regretted, 'she's always had these pathetic conventional ambitions, but I hoped she'd see beyond them eventually. Instead, they've won. A safe job, and a centrally heated flat with fitted carpets and modern plumbing – it's all she cares about.' He shook his shining golden head, genuinely bewildered.

It was no more than the truth, Emily knew. She knew, too, what Carmel thought of Greg's attitude. He and his social-work students, she argued, would have a totally different approach to the squalor they embraced so passionately if they'd been raised in Brixton instead of in affluent suburbia. 'In Brixton, see, you know you've got to escape. You must get educated and get out, find yourself a job that isn't on an alleyway to nowhere. These middle-class dropouts, they make me tired.'

A great divide yawned. Emily, optimistically, tried to bridge it with words, only to be shouted down.

One of the social-work students summed it up. 'You're as bad as she is, Emily,' she said. 'With your prissy office job, typing away all day, and your nice clean shirts.'

'What do you imagine you're achieving, anyway, by smoking pot, going without baths, getting up at noon, and wearing filthy old patched denim?' Emily retorted smartly. These days she took no lip from anyone. During her months in London, too, straddling three worlds as she found herself, she'd been forced to take her head out of the clouds and evaluate her own personal attitudes, and now her sympathy was one hundred per cent with Carmel. Greg might look fabulous, but inside that golden head was a load of claptrap. Melissa could have him.

Her contribution to the discussion came next, and put everything else out of Emily's mind.

'If Carmel's room is going free,' she suggested blithely, 'couldn't Em take it over?'

'Yes, I suppose so, if she wants it,' Greg agreed with his usual vague amiability, turning his blank blue gaze briefly on Emily.

She could only gape at him.

'Do you?' he asked impatiently.

Melissa answered for her. 'Of course she does. As it is she does nothing but travel back and forth in the Underground. Dreadfully tiring for her. Expensive, too.'

Emily stared.

'It worries me so much,' Melissa continued. 'Now if she could have Carmel's room it would be perfect for her. Think of the money and the time you'd save, Em – only a minute or two and you'd be in the hospital, instead of dragging about half over London morning and evening.'

Emily set her lips. Her thoughts were in chaos, but one fact predominated. This could possibly be Melissa's way of getting rid of her. Were she and Andrew tired of sharing the penthouse with her, week after week, and this a convenient method of ousting her without hurt feelings?

Working this out, she lost track of the conversation. She had one instinct only – at all costs to hide her dismay. The entire household in Knightsbridge were close to her now – even cross old Anna had accepted her, turned out to be not half bad. Most of all, though, there was Barnaby. Suddenly, though, at a casual suggestion from Melissa this evening, that way of life receded into the past. No more breakfasts with Barnaby and Joan, no more sleepy taxi rides in the early hours with Melissa, no comfortable sessions in the big living room after dinner, drinking Anna's superb coffee and chatting idly. As of now, the penthouse had ceased to be home. Determined no one should know how much she minded, she raised no objection to the plans Greg and Melissa were busily making on her behalf. Of course, she reminded herself firmly, Melissa was quite right about the travel. To walk into the Central each day would be pleasant.

She could move in on Saturday, as soon as Carmel moved out, Melissa was saying. That would give her the weekend to settle in. 'Buy yourself a nice sleeping bag,' she suggested enthusiastically. 'You can have a pillow, of course, and sheets and towels from home. I'll bring them over myself, help you to get organised.'

Carmel, told of the plan when Emily ran into her in the canteen, was nonplussed. Apologetic, too. 'I'm sorry, Em,' she said, worried. 'But I'll be taking the camp bed and my cupboard. I can't possibly afford to leave them behind for you. Will you be all right?'

'It's OK. Greg's found me a spare bed from No. 5 – a bit rickety, but it'll do me fine.'

'What are you going to keep your stuff in? You must keep everything locked up or those damned kids will knock them off the minute you turn your back.'

That this was the truth Emily knew from bitter experience. She had already lost a sweater, a pair of jeans, and two pairs of tights.

'Have you a case with a good lock?'

'I suppose I can bring my big case. That locks.'

'Do that, then. If I had my way, those kids wouldn't know what had hit them. But that wet Greg . . . ' She shrugged. 'I tell you, girl. I sure am thankful to be leaving that place.'

At No. 4, it appeared, they were equally thankful to see the back of her. 'I'm afraid,' even the good-humoured Susan remarked sadly, 'Carmel has turned out not to be a very *caring* sort of person.'

'No,' William agreed. 'We thought she'd be so useful with the West Indian children. But she makes no attempt at understanding their problems, simply threatens to thump them when they misbehave.'

On Saturday afternoon, progressing a little erratically along St Anne's Square with a rolled sleeping bag in polythene under one arm, her case in the other, Emily met James.

He relieved her of the case. 'Where are you off to?' he enquired.

'To No. 4.' She explained about her move.

He stared blankly. 'You're *what*? You mean to say . . . ?' She repeated the gist of her story.

'You're intending to sleep there permanently?'

'Yes.' Emily was brief. The pavement seemed no place to enter into an explanation of the fact that any intentions were Melissa's rather than her own, quite apart from her doubt as to whether she wanted to share this information with anyone.

'But, good grief, Em, you can't – hell.' He looked at his watch. 'Blast. I can't talk now. And tomorrow I have to drive down to Surrey to see a patient – I tell you what, we can have a chat over breakfast, how would that be?'

'Lovely.'

James, however, found nothing lovely in the situation. His day had gone cold and dark. Unjustifiably, prompted partly by the slight hesitation and evasiveness Emily was display-ing, he leapt to the conclusion that she'd moved in order to be near Matthew. He'd experienced spasms of jealousy of Matthew for months past, and now he was miserably certain Emily was on the point of living with him.

After he'd been to the hospital he returned to his flat and spent an unhappy evening, writing up his notes and arguing with himself. He had no evidence, after all. He shouldn't jump to conclusions like this.

Was Em even on the pill?

He stood up, tramped furiously round the flat. What the hell had any of this to do with him?

So he loved her. Always would. But he couldn't live her life for her.

She was so young, though. Only seventeen.

No, he was wrong. She was eighteen now, he'd taken her out to a celebration meal himself, and there'd been a party in the King's Head first.

The first he'd known about it, he remembered, had been when he went into the office to sign his letters and saw all the birthday greetings displayed on her desk. As far as he could see, everyone in the unit except for himself and Northiam had sent her a card. There were brightly coloured little parcels among the cards, too.

'I'm not opening them until six o'clock,' she had explained, looking up over the pile of letters she was sorting for him.

'Six o'clock?' Briefly he withdrew his attention from the details of Mrs Macpherson's mitral valvotomy. 'Why six?'

'Mark's standing me a birthday drink in the King's Head, and Sara and Bill are coming, and Wendy – you will, won't you? – and perhaps –'

'Am I invited?'

'Of course you are. I didn't think you'd be free. But please do come.'

In the end he'd been late, after all – but then so had Mark. They'd arrived together, to find Wendy's pathologist husband had already bought Emily her birthday drink, and the presents had been opened, were most of them already being worn. Long strings of beads, chosen carefully by Sara to go with Emily's shirts, matching bangles from Wendy, make-up, bath salts, toilet water, a pottery mug from Mark. Nothing, of course, from James.

So he'd blatantly pulled rank and invited her to a meal,

and had seen Mark's disappointment with undiluted joy. He and Emily had walked to Rules in Maiden Lane through back streets from the King's Head, and arrived hungry and invigorated, to eat roast beef and drink claret. It was then she'd told him she'd never had so many birthday parties – he could see her now, in a blue check shirt, with the blue beads and bangle that had been among her gifts, ticking off the celebrations on the fingers of one hand, and looking at him with those huge brown eyes of hers brimming with laughter. First, she'd enumerated, the King's Head, that evening. Second, this dinner with him. Third, a meal the previous evening in Greg's basement – barbecue chicken and frozen peas from Greg, and Yugoslav Riesling from Matthew, a carton of crisps thrown in. Fourth, Andrew and Melissa were to take her to the Hilton, and, fifth, there was to be a tea party with Barnaby on Saturday afternoon with a cake baked by Anna and eighteen candles at Barnaby's insistence.

After the meal he'd apologised to her – no card, no present.

'But, James, you've given me this super meal.' She'd meant it, he could see that. But it wasn't enough.

'No, I'd like to get you something.'

She'd protested again, but he was determined, though amazingly helpless. What could he buy for her? What would she like? Suddenly the purchase became important to him, he wanted almost desperately, ridiculous though it seemed, to buy her something she'd use every day, that he'd see her wearing. Like those beads. Or at least carrying. And that gave him the answer. He saw her bag, scuffed and shabby. He'd find her a good leather bag.

The next day he'd sought Felicity out in her laboratory and demanded her assistance. She gave it at once – making a mental note, of course, to pass all the details on to Northiam at the first opportunity. 'Heal's,' she said. 'We can walk across before lunch. I saw some fabulous bags there the other day.'

'I thought it was a furniture store.'

Felicity, as usual, was right – an attribute she shared with Northiam, of course. They chose an outrageously expensive sling bag of pale hide, and afterwards swallowed wholemeal rolls with skim-milk cheese and chives, drank coffee, at the Cranks lunch bar on the pavement outside, while the traffic roared by.

Out of the blue, Felicity remarked, 'Hang on to her, James, won't you?'

'Er – you mean Em?'

'Yes. Grab her and keep her. Don't let anything separate you, no matter what you have to do.'

He didn't know what to say. He remembered Felicity with Tom Rennison in the old days, remembered too how they'd all felt she'd been too proud to chase after him when he'd had to leave the Central, and his heart ached for her.

But what would Felicity expect him to do now? Emily was eighteen, of age. She could do as she pleased. No one could stop her living in the Dormobile with Matthew if she wanted to, and whatever Felicity might choose to believe, there was nothing he could do to put a stop to it.

He swore, and went back to the hospital, where he did a ferociously bad-tempered round, to the astonishment of the night staff.

On Sunday morning Emily arrived smiling and relaxed, and he hadn't the strength to embark on the grandfatherly interrogation he'd planned overnight. The sun shone brightly into the little kitchen, as they ate at the formica-topped table. At least he could give her a square meal, if nothing else, and he heaped her plate with bacon, eggs, mushrooms and tomatoes.

Emily ate greedily. She was pleased with life, and already coming round to the notion of living in St Anne's Square. There'd be problems, no doubt of that. But at last she was genuinely independent. To leave the penthouse almost without warning had been a shock, but now that she came to think it out she hadn't expected to live in the shelter provided by Melissa and Andrew indefinitely. The younger sister.

No more. From today she was an independent working woman with a room of her own. An off-beat room, if not grotty, and there were aspects of life in No. 4 which worried her more than a little. Like baths, for instance. Even so, the little attic, however primitive, had charm, and when she had bought some cheap cotton for curtains, scrounged boxes for shelves and a bedside table – well, then it would be her own place. She could have done with some heating in it, of course, and a means of cooking. But she wouldn't necessarily stay long – Carmel had moved on, and she would very likely do the same. She had made a beginning. And in the meantime it was great to be able to have breakfast with James. She buttered more toast greedily, and drank some of the excellent coffee.

'Heaven,' she said, sighing with satisfaction. 'They can't make toast, you know, at No. 4. No gas or electricity. Tinned milk, too, because of not having a refrigerator.'

'Why have you moved in there?' The enquiry came abruptly.

Emily picked her words carefully. She didn't want James to gain the impression that she and Melissa had had a row, or any sort of major disagreement. 'Well, you see, Melissa thought it would be easier if I was in St Anne's Square, instead of travelling backwards and forwards every day.'

'Oh.' James was taken aback. 'Not your idea, then?'

'No.' After all, it hadn't been, so why should she lie about it? 'But I'm not sorry, now I'm actually there.'

The words told James more than she bargained for. He saw at once that he'd been wrong about Matthew. Instead Melissa, egotistic and selfish as ever, was behind the move. He was furious.

To arrange to have Emily living permanently in the attic at No. 4, while Greg inhabited the basement, would suit Melissa very well. Emily, she would be able to inform everyone, had moved to a room near the hospital, and she, sisterly and affectionate, would, of course, keep popping over to see her, might well be expected to stay with her overnight. As usual, blind to all except her own desires, Melissa had probably not even noticed what she was doing to Emily.

He'd have to find something else for her. In a week or two he ought to be able to unearth some more suitable room for her than that attic in No. 4, and in the meantime he'd keep an alert eye on her, and take her out to as many meals as possible, fill her up with good-quality protein and vitamins. Or this was how he put it to himself, though somewhere in his consciousness a plan formed that had very little to do with proteins, amino-acids and vitamins A to K. What he was cherishing inwardly was a series of vignettes, of himself and Emily, dressed to kill and out on the town. They were gazing into one another's eyes across candlelit tables, holding hands as they strolled by the gleaming river at night, drinking coffee as they sat – could it be entwined? – on his big sofa.

Looking ahead to this glorious future, he smiled at her, and she smiled back. Both of them had the utmost confidence in what lay ahead.

6. In The Small Hours

The transition each evening from the centrally heated hospital to the penetrating damp and icy chill of the shabby, down-at-heel terrace houses was hard to take. Emily sent home for her ribbed woollen tights, thick fisherman's sweater and a long padded skirt she'd made herself a couple of years earlier, but had never imagined she'd need in London.

One dark and freezing evening she arrived to find Matthew lugging a bag of Coalite down the area steps. 'I'm tired of that stinking oil stove,' he told her. 'Tonight we'll have a real fire.'

A fire, crackling in the grate of the old range. Emily's eyes shone, and her face was alive with delight. Matthew, who'd already dumped his bag on the hearth, and was watching her – a recent habit of his – found himself caught up in a torrent of desire for her slim vivid beauty. He reminded himself – another recent habit – of Jackie at home in Sydney. But surely she'd never discover if he had another girl in London, would she? And what the eye doesn't see the heart doesn't grieve over, he reminded himself – a more comforting reminder, this, than those he'd had earlier. 'Em,' he began – he really couldn't help himself – 'you grow more beautiful every blooming day, y'know that?' His lean height armoured in his vast Afghan coat that sprouted sheepskin from every seam, he put out long arms and enfolded her securely.

Now, Emily addressed herself firmly, it was beginning. A thrilling sexy affair with Matthew.

But where was the thrill? Absent. To her intense disappointment her only reaction to his embrace, which, after all, she'd been half-expecting for weeks, was to register with extreme distaste the smell of inadequately cured sheepskin mingled with paraffin and stale sweat. She tried to ignore this, think instead of how fond of Matthew she was, and, above all, whip up some passion. Melissa had been advising her for some weeks past to shack up with him. 'Why don't you? You've got to begin sometime, and he obviously fancies you.' Certainly there was nothing Emily wanted – or so she had supposed – more than to be shot of her juvenile virginity. 'No strings,' Melissa added. 'He'll be going home to his Australian bird next year, so you won't get stuck with him interminably. And he's a great guy.'

Surely, now that the relationship between them was about to take off, she wasn't going to retreat because his sheepskin coat ponged? Could she perhaps be under-sexed, or something awful like that? Why was she unresponsive and, to be strictly truthful, more bored than anything else, when this long streak of genuine Aussie charm seized her so promisingly?

Matthew had his own explanation. 'My poor little Em, you're freezing,' he told her. 'Wait a jiffy and I'll have this fire going and warm you up in no time.' With a crescendo of clattering and banging, he started to clear out the grate.

Emily, again to her surprise, had to clench her teeth on an overwhelming impulse to inform him that even if she did happen to be petrified with cold, she was not his poor little Em. Nor anyone else's. Poor little Em. She gritted her teeth with fury, and, mainly in order to release some of this pent-up emotion as well as to give herself a chance to work out what she was going to do about Matthew, she in her turn clattered round the basement room, lighting candles to augment the light that came in through the dirty window from the street lamp outside, clearing away the debris of the previous evening's supper, heating water on the Camping Gaz burners, taking rubbish to the dustbins. The room remained freezing, and she kept her coat on, reminding herself uneasily that unless she quickly went upstairs to change, in the morning her clothes were going to be smelling very

86

much like Matthew's. Northiam would probably turn her out.

On the other hand, if she cleared off now, Matthew might be hurt, might imagine she intended to snub him. A quiet inner voice commented acidly that this would be a splendid solution, but Emily told it to shut up.

Matthew had reached the stage of putting a match to his firelighters. Flames began to roar, and the room, with the fire and the candles alight, looked cheerful and welcoming. Emily, instead of going upstairs to change, made coffee and crouched down with Matthew on the floor in front of the ancient range to drink it.

To her secret relief, the first of the students appeared, followed by Greg and Melissa, and soon they were all drinking instant coffee in front of the fire, at last giving out a good heat. Coffee was followed by the evening meal. Greg produced two tins of beans and a wrapped loaf, one of the students had a tin of soup, Emily contributed eggs, and Matthew had bought sausages. The frying pan sizzled, blue smoke filled the air. Too late, Emily remembered she was still in her office gear.

In fact, what with dodging Matthew and talking to Melissa, it was not until after midnight that she finally climbed the long flights of stairs, carrying her torch, and thinking of her lonely bed in the cold little attic. Never had she been more pleased with her own company. She was worried that she felt like this, half-ashamed still of her lack of desire. All right, so Matthew didn't turn her on. But could this mean she was unturnonable?

Her mind preoccupied with this argument with herself, the emptiness of her attic room failed to strike her immediately. And then she came to. The place was extraordinarily bare. Where was her sleeping bag? Her suitcase? Surely, they couldn't be missing? She stared round her in bewilderment.

The room remained bare and empty. Only the rickety old camp bed occupied it, its dirty canvas showing every stain. No sleeping bag spread over it. Even her pillow had disappeared.

A sensation of disbelief fought with the cold that began to seep right through into her bones.

Surely she could not be standing here, alone, at one o'clock in the morning, all her possessions missing?

Stolen? Carmel had often warned her this might happen. Now it had, and worst of all, as she had so carefully locked everything up – Carmel's advice again – the thieves had walked off with her case. No doubt they proposed to break into it at their leisure. And now she was left without even a sleeping bag. In fact, except for what was in her sling bag and in her desk in the office, it looked as though she had lost everything.

The situation seemed ridiculous. Incredible, too. She flashed her torch round the room again, in disbelief. Up and down the blank walls – painted apple-green by Carmel, who had hung cherry red curtains at the small window. All bare. One rickety camp bed. No more. Only one thing for it. Downstairs again to the warm basement, to tell Melissa and Greg what had happened. Greg would find her an old sleeping bag – one that wasn't worth stealing – from next door.

That would look after tonight.

Tomorrow was another day.

Back down the four flights. At the top of the basement stairs she paused. She could hear quiet, loving voices, soft and intimate. At once she felt she was intruding.

Silly to feel so awkward. They wouldn't mind, when they heard what had happened. But she ought at least to call out, to warn them she was on the way down. Otherwise it would be embarrassing for all of them. She opened her mouth to call out to Melissa. And shut it again. It was embarrassing already. Their talk was so very explicit. A cry of pure joy came, too. Triumphant, and followed by other sounds, from Melissa this time, and more talk.

Talk that had nothing to do with her. That she should never have overheard.

And so, once again, as she had done months earlier on that first morning in St Anne's Square, Emily retreated. Shivering, she stood in the hall.

Suppose she came crashing down the basement stairs like

half an army on the march, banging and yelling, so that they couldn't be taken by surprise?

No good. She couldn't do it. To interrupt them now was impossible. She'd heard too much. She'd have to freeze until morning.

Well, she could last out the night, surely? She wasn't an invalid or an elderly person. She had a roof over her head, no more than a few hours to get through.

In the morning, she'd find out what had happened, deal with her problems.

In the morning, OK. But what now?

A sudden gleam of hope. Perhaps her things hadn't been stolen at all. Someone might have moved them for her to the big first-floor dormitory, then forgotten to tell her about it. That would be the explanation. She'd panicked too soon.

She climbed the first flight of stairs again, looked into the large L-shaped room with its balcony overlooking the square where the students camped out. Once the drawing room of the old house, in more prosperous days, there was a fluted chimney-piece with a basket grate, and the original tall Georgian windows with their wooden shutters, closed now against the freezing night air.

Earlier, the students had taken a shovelful of glowing coals from the range to light a fire for themselves in the grate here. Perhaps one of them was away, and they found they had a spare bed and decided it would be warmer for her here than in the attic. They were all so vague, it would be exactly like them to overlook the small matter of informing her.

The fire had gone out. Emily hesitated to flash her torch here and there, in case she woke them. A glimmer of light, though, came in through the cracks between the shutters from the street lamp outside, and as her eyes grew accustomed to the gloom, she could distinguish, amid the usual chaos of scattered clothes, tote bags, cases, empty cartons and boxes that constituted furniture, humped forms on each bed, out for the count. There was an all-pervasive smell in the room, too. Not dry rot, or unwashed human beings. Pot. After three months Emily had no difficulty in recognising it, and she understood at once why they'd left the basement unusually early. They'd been sitting round their own fire sharing a joint.

Well, that settled it. If they'd been smoking pot, they'd never have been bothered as to whether she might be cold up in the attic. Even so, she examined the room, flashing her torch around freely, knowing they wouldn't wake.

Nothing. By now she hadn't supposed there would be. Still, she'd look right through the house.

Methodically, though with little hope, she checked the remaining rooms – or those of them with doors that opened. Some of them had already been boarded up by the council. Those she could see into were a misery, with window panes missing, shutters hanging, floorboards broken and sprouting fungus. They smelt not of pot, but of mould, mildew, decay.

No one had moved her case and her sleeping bag as part of some idiotic joke, as she had briefly imagined. Instead her first conclusion had been correct. They had been stolen. In the morning, she was sure, Greg would advise her what to do, and sort out the kids, who were bound to be responsible for her loss. In the meantime, though, she was unable to stop shivering. Futile to suppose she could drop off to sleep in her clothes on the camp bed, under no more than her own coat.

Nothing else for it. She'd have to pull herself together, go down and face Greg and Melissa.

In the hall she paused again, hating the prospect of the final flight, hating the necessity of appealing to them.

Another face came, unbidden, to her mind.

Matthew.

Outside in the Dormobile.

He pretended – to the council, and the fuzz, and the office at the London School of Economics – that he slept in No. 4, which he always gave as his official address. But as for spending a night under its roof – not Matthew. The Dormobile was not only his transport, his storehouse, his study and his snack bar, it was also his bedroom.

She opened the front door, looked at the Dormobile parked outside. So easy to go in with Matthew, who wouldn't be in the least annoyed if she woke him. On the contrary, he'd welcome her with open arms. Not a doubt of it.

7. James

Emily's trouble was, she didn't, now or ever, want Matthew to welcome her with open arms.

What she wanted was somewhere to sleep, not a running fight with a sexy Aussie, least of all a hectic night of love in a Dormobile. Maybe she was frigid, under-sexed, anything you like. But at this precise moment what she longed for most of all was somewhere warm to lie down, where she would be able, preferably in clean sheets, to go to sleep. Just that. No more. Even better would be the sort of room everyone but Carmel despised, with central heating, wall to wall carpeting, and a bathroom next door with lashings of hot water.

Emily's feet had it worked out. They knew all the answers. They set off briskly down the steps, away from the Dormobile, up the square towards the house where James had his flat. At this point Emily asserted herself. Her self-willed feet might lead her to James's front door, but that was as far as they were allowed to go. Emily's hands, under stricter discipline, refrained from beating the frenzied tattoo on the knocker that the small primitive animal within her depths was crying out for.

Emily, the adult Emily that is, weary but refusing to give up, independent at whatever cost, bullied her recalcitrant feet into walking on. She knew what she was going to do. She would pick up a taxi, cross London to Knightsbridge, spend the remainder of the night in the penthouse. Simple. Why on earth had this easy solution not occurred to her earlier?

By far the most likely place to pick up a taxi at this hour would be the hospital. The night porter would have the number, wouldn't even consider her request strange – he'd assume she'd been to a late party somewhere.

She walked, purposefully now, between the blocks, came to the lighted entrance, which, if not exactly Piccadilly Circus in the rush hour, was certainly not deserted or silent. No longer alone, part of the hospital again, exactly as if this was a problem of her working day, Emily knew she could cope. And with this slackening of tension, her mind began to function – and at once came up with a snag. All very well to decide to go to the penthouse, fine for her, but what was she going to say to Anna and Joan? How could she explain to them that when her possessions had been stolen – from this new flat (for so her sister had labelled it) that Melissa had obligingly found for her – far from consulting her, she had come, alone, in a taxi at three in the morning across London to Knightsbridge, leaving her sister sleeping in the mythical flat?

Emily knew exactly what they'd assume. What was more, they'd be right.

She'd have blown Melissa's cover.

Her all-knowing feet came to her rescue again, walked past the porter's lodge, along the corridors towards the cardio-thoracic department. Of course, this was the answer. She could sit quietly in her own office. It would be warm, she'd soon thaw out, might even snooze on a chair, and then go to the canteen for an early breakfast, wash and tidy herself in the cloakroom, start the day's work in a civilised manner.

If anyone came into the office – a nurse, say, or one of the house surgeons, to leave a message or deposit a tape, she'd simply pretend she'd left her pen, or her make-up bag. Anything would do. Quite why she should be searching for these objects at three in the morning was none of their business, after all. And with any luck they wouldn't, if they were on night duty, notice the time.

She turned the door handle, walked in.

Sitting at Wendy's desk, talking into the microphone of the dictating machine, was James. He'd been, in fact, called to a patient in intensive care, and, while waiting for his treatment to take effect, had slipped down to the office to clear some of his outstanding correspondence. He stopped in mid-sentence. 'What on earth are you doing here?'

'I came to look for my pen,' Emily said unconvincingly.

'The pen of your aunt, I suppose.' James was sardonic, though inwardly he was furious. What the hell did Em think she was doing, roaming round the hospital in the middle of the night with crazy excuses? This was what came of letting her loose in that abode of drop-outs.

His cutting voice, and the bleak look he turned on her, finished Emily. Fighting the quaver in her voice, she mumbled indistinctly that she was very sorry, James, but she had had enough. 'I'm sorry, but I really have.' She gulped, and to her annoyance, tears began to roll down her cheeks.

James's arms came round her, and she seemed, though quite how she had arrived there she had no recollection, to be sitting on his knee, crying damply into his shirt. This was amazingly comforting and almost immediately she felt much better, pushed her hair back out of her face, and explained reasonably coherently what had happened.

She left a gap, between arriving at the top of the basement stairs after discovering her loss, and arriving at the Central. James was quite able to interpret this for himself, but all he said was 'We can't go on discussing it here. We'll go along to my place.'

They went out through the main entrance again, walked along the square and up to his flat. Here he sat her down on the sofa, switched on all three bars of the electric fire, and presented her with a large brandy. 'You'll have to spend the rest of the night here,' he said curtly. 'Tomorrow I'll find you somewhere to stay. If Wendy wasn't on holiday, so that I know the office would be a shambles if Sara was left on her own, I'd pack you straight off home to Herefordshire.'

This was too much. Emily rallied her flagging forces. 'Oh no, you wouldn't,' she told him snappishly, chin raised, eyes indomitable.

Unexpectedly, he smiled affectionately. 'Never give up, do you, love?' he asked.

The smile, and the tenderness in his voice, warmed Emily

through to her bones, and she smiled back, her heart in her eyes now, so that James caught his breath. 'I'm not going home,' she reiterated, her voice quivering between laughter and another bout of tears. 'And no male chauvinist is going to order me there. That's final.' She gulped an immoderate amount of brandy, spluttered wildly, and felt for a handkerchief, gasping and choking.

James passed her one, and smiled at her again. His faded blue eyes were softness itself, and the warmth in Emily's bones spread, was somehow succeeding in unwinding the tight knot located in her uneasy stomach. She relaxed, leant back against the sofa cushions, and smiled back at him with absolute trust.

'Listen, Em,' he said gently. He took her hand, and as he did so she felt reassurance flood through her. She settled herself thankfully against his shoulder. He would see to everything, and all she had to do now was to lean back and let him. For ever, if necessary. 'Next week,' he was telling her placidly, 'Wendy will be back. She and Sara can manage in the office then. You can go home, while I sort this nonsense out and find you somewhere reasonable to live.'

At that moment she wanted nothing more than to give in, longed only to please him by agreeing to do whatever he asked. Anything so that she could stay there with him, cherished and protected. Instead she took a deep breath, said 'No'. She had to force the word out. 'I'm staying in London,' she added. The final sentence took all her remaining energy.

'We'll talk about it in the morning,' he said. Against his shoulder he could feel her quivering, shaking with nerves. The shock of her loss, as well as of what must have been lonely, anguished hours, was with her still, he thought, and he took her, as he might have done a small child in the ward, into comforting arms, stroked her hair, held her and patted her, murmuring soft endearments, quiet encouraging nothings. Soothing her in his arms, slowly and steadily he repeated that all would be well, there was nothing now to worry about. He was giving her what in the ward would have been routine reassurance – the years, after all, had given him endless opportunities to practise this art. But what he added, for Emily alone, was his love, and even though he used no phrases to tell her of this, it came through to her, strong and sure, so that she relaxed at last. Lying back against his chest, feeling his heart beating steadily away, she was carried on a flood tide of security into a sense of overwhelming peace.

She had no notion how fragile her peace was.

James might have begun by treating her like a child in the ward, but she was no child, and his body knew it. He stood up. 'You'd better get some sleep.'

'Yes,' she agreed vaguely, warm and drowsy and content, and there, it was plain, for the taking.

'Have a bath.' He was peremptory. 'That'll make sure you're really warm through. Come on.' He led the way towards the bathroom, pausing at the airing cupboard to haul out towels and sheets.

She followed him obediently, took them from him.

He opened the door to the small spare room. 'Can you look after yourself now, do you think? I must go back to intensive care.'

'Yes, I'm fine,' she said sleepily.

He kissed her, and then, suddenly, he was gone, the front door thudding behind him. Emily went dreamily into the bathroom, began running the bath. Clouds of steam rose into the air, and she viewed the phenomenon with sleepy approval. Exactly as she'd imagined. Since she'd had no more than half the brandy James had poured for her, she fetched it and took the glass into the bath with her. What with exhaustion and alcohol, she was now distinctly high, and lay smiling to herself. Every cloud had a silver lining. She'd lost all she possessed, but somehow she'd landed up lolling in a hot bath in James's flat swigging about half a pint of brandy. James had kissed her, too, she hadn't been too bemused to appreciate that. Something had changed between them. Something new and important had come into their relationship. What it was she was too sleepy to know, but tomorrow she'd work it out.

Tomorrow, though, was back to square one. 'This weekend I'm going to take a day off and drive you home,' James announced, pouring coffee and sounding like her elderly uncle. 'You can explain what's been happening to your parents, and sort out with them whether you should come back to the Central or not, and if so, where you'll stay. You can't go on like this.'

'I'm not going home,' Emily said flatly. The knot came back to her stomach. Could he make her? Surely not. 'I don't want to, for one thing, and in any case I can't possibly just clear off. You know perfectly well I can't.'

'They'll manage without you,' he said brusquely. 'They've done it before.'

But they weren't going to do it again, not if she knew it. 'I'm not going,' she repeated. 'You can't seriously expect me to walk out, creep home to Mummy and Daddy like a spoilt baby, all because a few of my belongings have been stolen.'

'Put like that,' he had to admit, 'I suppose it does seem a bit feeble. You'll have to go back to Knightsbridge, that's all.'

'Oh, I can't – Melissa – I mean, I don't think – ' This was deep water, and Emily was thankful for the interruption of the telephone. When James finished his conversation, she was ready to leave, and he had no opportunity to ask more questions, instead simply arranged hurriedly to meet her here at his flat for the evening meal.

In the office she sniffed suspiciously at her garments, and as soon as Sara walked in demanded 'Can you smell me? Is it awful? Do I smell hopelessly of frying?'

Sara, clean as a whistle in a new olive-green overdress with a gleaming white polo-neck beneath it, and skin-tight shiny leather boots that Emily coveted, sniffed obediently. 'I can a bit,' she admitted.

Emily began to pour out her story, but the telephone rang, and when she came off it Sara was already typing from one of James's tapes. 'Can't stop,' she apologised. 'He's left a note. He wants to sign these immediately after the ward round. You'll have to tell me later – can you go and fetch the post?'

In her lunch hour Emily rushed over to No. 5 to catch Greg and tell him what had happened the night before, and then galloped back to the Central to find Sara dealing with a new load of tapes brought in by Mark. It was not until they were drinking their tea that she finally had a chance to tell her about the theft.

'You mean you've lost everything?'

Emily nodded.

'Whatever are you going to do? How's your cash balance?'

Emily grimaced.

'Can't you borrow from your sister?'

'I don't want to.'

Sara gave her a quick glance, but once again the telephone rang, and at last the end of the day came before they'd had a chance to plan any action.

'I'm dreadfully sorry, Em, but I must run,' Sara said. 'I'm meeting Bill. You do pong rather of frying, you know – the central heating brings it out. Thank God Northiam didn't show up today. I tell you what, I'll lend you something to-morrow. I'll look something out, and bring it in with me. An old mini, or something like that, that won't show you're a minute size ten and I'm the original beanpole plus.'

'Angel. I can ring up my Mum, get her to send off a few tatty old garments, too, like sweaters, and my horrible old school mack.'

'If my tights wouldn't be yards too long, I'd lend you some – runs and all. Heavens, I must get a move on, or Bill's going to be livid. I suppose you've told the police, by the way?'

'I haven't actually.' Emily was uneasy. 'When I saw Greg at lunchtime, you see, he said –'

'Don't be daft, Em. Of course you must report it. Look, I simply can't wait now. Ask James, though. He'll tell you.'

That James would tell her, of course, was hardly news to Emily, and sure enough, when they met that evening, he was shocked to learn that she had not so far reported the theft, and at once offered to go with her to the police station. 'Before supper,' he added firmly.

'Oh no, James, I can't,' Emily protested. 'I saw Greg, and he pointed out –'

James swore luridly, and told Emily what Greg could do with himself.

'But, James –'

'It's nothing to do with him. It's your belongings that have gone missing, not his. Come on.'

'I can't. I really can't. I promised Greg –'

'*What* did you promise him?'

'He thinks he can find out from the kids themselves who took my case – even he admits it must have been one of them. He says' – Emily knew what James's reaction was going to be, and advanced Greg's opinion gingerly – 'he says whoever it was must be more disturbed than he realised, and is going to need a great deal of individual attention.'

James didn't swear again, which was what Emily was expecting. He stared, and began to shake with laughter, finally, chuckling, remarked only, 'He's a nut case, that's all there is to it. Right round the twist.'

'He does have some fairly down-to-earth reasons for not wanting the police called in,' Emily felt compelled to say. 'The Council, according to him, are already looking for an excuse to close the hostel down. Having the police in would give them their opportunity, and make life much more difficult for William, so as Greg feels badly enough as it is about leaving him –'

'So in order to ease his own guilty conscience, he's proposing that you should lose everything and say nothing? It's too bad of him, Em. Time he faced up to his own problems and their consequences.' His expression changed. 'All right, love, not to worry. We'll let him get away with bloody murder if it makes you feel better.' He kissed her, held her to him for a brief moment that was gone almost before she knew it had happened. 'Em,' he said, out of the blue, his words coming very slow and sure, 'what happens to you matters very much to me. Don't forget, will you?'

As if she could. She mattered to James. She was so occupied in savouring his statement – she'd treasure what he'd just said for ever, she knew – that she didn't answer him. It didn't, in any case, enter her head that he might expect some sort of response.

'So don't take risks, will you?' he went on, after a second's pause.

'What sort of risks, for goodness' sake?' She was genuinely puzzled.

'Like living in that dump,' he said morosely. 'However, I'll agree that going off now and reporting the loss of your case isn't in the least likely to get it back for you. So we'll call it a day, shall we, and go and eat?'

'Oh, James, I would be so thankful. If we could just forget about it, and –'

'On one condition. I'll make a deal with you. If we leave matters as they are, I want you to promise me that whatever happens, you'll not under any circumstances spend another night in that house.'

Emily began to protest, but James ignored her. 'Tonight you must go back to Knightsbridge, understood? After that, I'll organise you a flat round here.'

Emily was incoherent with delight. 'You?' she said. 'Here? Me?' She hugged him. 'When?'

'In a day or two. I'll find something. I ought to have seen to it before.'

'Oh no. I ought to be able to find places for myself.'

'You'll go back to Knightsbridge tonight, then, and stay there until I've found somewhere.'

'I don't quite know what Melissa's going to say.'

'I'll talk to her.' His jaw snapped shut. 'Now we'll go and eat.'

She followed him downstairs and out into the square. On this occasion it was her hands which seemed to be leading a life of their own, hanging on to James's arm like a lifeline. What had happened to her independence?

They arrived at Giovanni's, opposite the hospital, where James had evidently decided they were going to eat. He had omitted to discuss the possibility with her, of course, but she sat meekly down where he indicated and let him order for her without a murmur. Plates piled high with tagliatelle verde and a bowl of cheese were placed before them, followed by veal in a sauce of mushrooms and peppers, with new potatoes and courgettes. They drank a chilled white Chianti and afterwards James ate a wedge of Camembert, while Emily, warm and replete and beginning to be drowsy –

99

only four hours' sleep the previous night, after all – toyed with a lemon water ice.

James finished his cheese, refused coffee for them both, and put her into the Jaguar. He drove across to Knightsbridge, stopped outside Oriel House. 'I'll come up with you,' he said. 'I want to have a few plain words with that sister of yours.'

They went together – hand in hand, to the vast interest of the night porter, who related the sight to Anna, nodding her head wisely over a cup of tea the next morning – through the entrance hall with the tawny carpet and the concrete saucers filled with greenery, and up in the hissing lift. Emily let them into the penthouse, where they were greeted by a smell of Italian cooking and Melissa's musk perfume.

'An early night for you,' James said annoyingly. 'You're asleep on your feet, love.' He pointed her shoulders down the hall and smacked her lightly on the bottom. 'Bed.'

Emily, who'd been hoping he might take it into his head to kiss her again, in which case she would, this time, have been ready for it, was far from pleased to find she was relegated to the status of Melissa's infant sister once again. 'Night,' she said grumpily, plodding off along the passage into her room.

James stared after her, shook his head, and went in search of Melissa. He found her extended full length on the white hide settee, in her harem trousers and a gauzy tunic top, turning the pages of American *Vogue* to soft music from the stereo speakers. Delighted to see him, she produced her slowest and most fascinating smile, stretched sinuously, and patted the settee invitingly. James sat down heavily in a chair. 'I want to talk to you seriously,' he began formidably.

Melissa was thrilled. After all these years, could it be that he loved her still? Was he hungering beyond all bearing for her, prepared even to deceive Andrew at last? 'Tell me at once, darling, what is it?' she cooed.

'About Em.'

'Em?' Melissa abandoned her pose, sat up abruptly. 'What's Em gone and done?' she demanded irritably.

'It's what you've gone and done,' James said stringently.

'Me? I've done nothing.' Melissa was genuinely bewildered.

'Oh, for Pete's sake, Melissa, try opening those zonking great eyes of yours and taking a look at what's going on in the world around you for once. You've been making use of Em, and it's got to stop. As of now.'

Andrew had accused her of much the same fault more than once, though usually in connection with her habit of expecting Emily to sit in for them during the evening, or look after Barnaby on Joan's day off. But how could a question like this be bothering James this evening?

He saw her blank expression. 'Suggesting she moved into that damned awful house in St Anne's Square, I mean.'

'But, James, she did nothing but travel backwards and forwards when she was living here. Dreadfully tiring, and I thought – '

'Baloney. You moved her in there to suit yourself. Simply to give you an alibi for meeting that idiot Greg – though why you should want to passes my comprehension.'

'Now you're jealous,' Melissa said, pleased, her confidence returning.

'I am not jealous. I'm angry. How can you be so irresponsible? It beats me. Don't you understand, fathead, that house is not only freezing cold but thoroughly unhygienic? Damp, too, and it's no thanks to you Em hasn't gone down with bronchitis. And quite apart from that, it's no place for a girl like Em. She'll tell you herself what happened last night – '

'Last night? But I was there myself, and – '

'And you hadn't a clue that anything happened. Exactly. That's what I mean. Now, Melissa, it's important. She's not to go back there. Understand? She'll have to sleep here until I find her somewhere near the Central, and you must see to it that she does. What you and Greg get up to is your affair, but if I find Em is sleeping in No. 4 again then I'll know I can't rely on you, and I'll have to talk to Andrew about the whole problem. I don't want to, of course. But I will if I have to. Got it?'

Melissa got it.

'So see to it that Em doesn't cross the threshold of that slum again, won't you?'

'Darling, you are being quite dreadfully unfair,' Melissa said mildly. 'But of course if you think living in No. 4 isn't good for Em, naturally I'll do my best to see she doesn't go there. If you were so worried about her I can't think why you didn't mention it before.'

Though neither of them said so, both of them knew James had won.

In the event, though, Emily remained at Knightsbridge for less than a week. Only two mornings later, when she arrived in the office, she found a note on her desk from James. He'd made enquiries, it informed her, and General Theatre Sister, Barbie Henderson, could let her have a bed-sitting room in her flat at No. 38. Emily was to ring her to make an appointment to see it.

Thankfully Emily telephoned, and Barbie Henderson invited her to come to look at the flat in her lunch hour.

Barbie turned out to be dark, in her early thirties, with a soft gentle expression and a quick smile. In the attics, her sitting room, with its sloping ceiling and windows overlooking the square, was charming, curtained in brown and white gingham, rush matting on the floor, comfortable chairs and sparse furniture in natural unstained woods. A country home in the centre of the city. The room she offered Emily had more of the rush matting, white-painted furniture, and curtains, cushions and divan cover in a flowery Laura Ashley print, the sloping walls painted a pale cinnamon. Emily liked it at once, and when she met James that evening she was able to tell him she was moving in on Sunday afternoon.

8. A White Christmas

No chance of hiding anything at the Central. Even before she had moved into No. 38, St Anne's Square with Barbie Henderson, word swept round the unit. James had planted young Em out with General Theatre Sister. What did this mean? A step on the road to matrimony?

In the cardio-thoracic unit, though Northiam was the figurehead – discussed, joked about, and feared more than the wrath of God – it was James who, in the eyes of the staff, actually ran the unit. And since they were all incessantly fascinated by one another's private lives, James and Emily provided as much food for gossip and speculation as did Northiam and Felicity.

The Northiam marriage, of course, had been a topic of unfailing interest long before the wedding day, and fresh evidence recently come to light was widely canvassed. Was the short-lived partnership already doomed? Northiam, it had leaked out, was in touch with an estate agent. He had been to look, it was rumoured, at a number of service flats in Harley Street. He'd been heard on the telephone talking about central heating, double-glazing, whether there was a restaurant, room service, and making appointments to view flats in various blocks. Up in the theatre one or two people insisted he'd specifically told them he was going to go across to Harley Street to look at a flat, and that afterwards he'd meet them in the ward.

Not everyone was in agreement that looking at service flats necessarily meant the break-up of the marriage. There was another school of thought which maintained that Northiam was in fact looking for consulting rooms rather than for a place to lay his solitary head, that for the first time in his illustrious career he proposed to enter private practice – the outcome, they asserted, of his row with the administration over the pacemakers.

James advanced a different theory, which everyone considered an intolerably dull interpretation of the wildly intriguing facts. It did so happen, of course, that James had been offered this explanation by Northiam himself – but then, there were plenty to point out, this was typical, simply another instance of crafty old Northiam up to his usual tricks, throwing dust in the eyes of any of his downtrodden staff who presumed to imagine they could begin to read his intentions. What Northiam alleged, in James's version, was that he felt Felicity to be overburdened. Running a home and a career was exhausting her. So they were giving up the house and moving into a service flat, as soon as they could find one that suited them.

Needless to say, this dull explanation satisfied no one except James.

However, if the Northiam marriage was on the edge of disintegration, there was no sign of this at Christmas. Northiam and Felicity held their usual enormous party in the St John's Wood house for half the hospital. Emily bought a new dress for the affair, on Sara's advice, of soft beige floating in envelope folds from the shoulders.

'Yuki again?' Felicity enquired, eye-catching herself in a cloud of drifting yellow.

'Marks & Spencer,' Emily said smugly. 'My very own dress, this time.'

'Terrific. I must go along there myself one lunch hour.'

Emily kept her mouth shut, though, as to the source of her new dress when Andrew and Melissa threw their Christmas party in the penthouse. Neither of them, she was well aware by now, would have been exactly pleased if she'd brandished her personal shopping habits before their well-heeled guests.

Barbie threw a party in the attic flat, crowds of surgeons, anaesthetists and sisters from general surgery. Two days later there was a cardio-thoracic party in James's flat, and then there was the nurses' dance, and the medical school dance, and an unofficial cardio-thoracic celebration which began unexpectedly one evening in the King's Head and adjourned to James's flat at closing time.

At all these junketings there were two main subjects of conversation, one of them known to Emily, but the other totally unsuspected. These two ever-interesting topics were the imminent collapse of the Northiam marriage and the equally imminent loss of Emily's virtue to James.

Ignorant of this forecast, which would have cheered her immensely, Emily went off home for the Christmas holiday, having extracted a promise from James that he would come down to Wistaria Lodge on Boxing Day. She herself went down by train with Barnaby, taking him to his grandparents two days before Christmas, while Melissa would drive down with Andrew on Christmas Eve when he returned from Zürich.

Valerie Goring was enchanted to have Emily and Barnaby to herself. She was less delighted, though, with Emily's appearance. 'You know,' she said irritably to her husband, 'that wretched Melissa can't have looked after her at all. She didn't have to do much, either – all the staff she has in that great flat of hers, she only needed to keep half an eye out for Em, see that she had a square meal each day and enough sleep. And obviously she's done neither. Em has lost far too much weight –'

'Only her puppy fat. And it suits her,' replied her doting father.

' – great shadows under her eyes.'

'Vast improvement in her looks, it seems to me. She's grown into a real dish.' Charles Goring preened. 'They'll all be after her at the Central, I shouldn't wonder. Too much gadding about with young men, that's what will have caused the shadows under her eyes.' He whistled wolfishly.

'Much you care if the poor child has gone hungry, as well as being worn out and short of sleep,' Valerie said disgustedly. 'That's of no consequence, apparently, so long as it renders her more attractive to your self-indulgent sex.'

'She'll lead some man a dance,' her father rejoined fondly. 'You should know about that, if anyone does, Valerie thought. Twenty years earlier she had been Charles Goring's practice secretary when Melissa's mother, Chloe, played him up all round the countryside, finally left him. Valerie, who had loved him throughout and had watched the disintegration of his marriage with mingled agony and hope, had never been able to forgive Chloe for the harm she'd done the serious young doctor she'd married and then abandoned.

For Christmas, Melissa had had her curls silvered, and, wearing a nineteen-twenties outfit of knitted silver lurex, drooping and fluid, that accentuated her height and slimness, and a silver chain with a huge rough-cut amethyst dangling almost to her knees – Andrew's present – she made the rest of the household look insignificant. Her father watched her, remembered Chloe, and drank his Christmas champagne – provided by his wealthy son-in-law – with mixed feelings.

Melissa was in a state of high excitement. Andrew had made, she informed them, a down payment on a Swiss chalet, and they were off to sample its delights early in the New Year.

'We may live there for half the year,' she told her awed family. 'It'll be as easy for Andrew to come to Zürich as London.'

'Fabulous,' Emily breathed.

'And we've decided it's time we added to our family,' Melissa added, casually.

'Yes,' Andrew agreed. 'Barnaby is beginning to get above himself.' He ruffled his son's dark head affectionately. 'He needs brothers and sisters.'

'We thought we'd have two more anyway,' Melissa mused maternally, bathing Barnaby in a warm glow of parental devotion.

Emily's jaw dropped. 'But what about – ?' Just in time she stopped. No one round the table knew even of the existence of Greg.

Round her the talk flowed on happily as they discussed the Swiss climate, communications, ski-ing in winter, alpine meadows in summer, mountain air and good food, cleanliness and comfort.

Only Charles Goring understood that a bribe had been

offered and accepted, and wondered, momentarily, if he had had the money whether he might have been able to manage Chloe in the same way. But then he would have missed Valerie, a nourishing second marriage, and Em. His darling Em, secretly his best-loved. He drained his glass, deciding he'd settle for life as it had turned out.

Boxing Day morning, and from the window of her room Emily stared out at the snow that blanketed the hills and lay several inches deep in the garden. The air was clear – no more snow likely to fall, she thought – the sun shone from a pale blue sky, glinting on snow crystals weighing down the branches of the trees, making blue shadows across the white lawn, and sparkling on the rutted drive. At any other time Emily's eyes would have dwelt with delight on this magic beauty. Now she was thinking only of James. Would the snow prevent him from joining them? Would the telephone ring at any minute now, and James be at the other end, saying that with the threat of more snow to come before nightfall he couldn't risk driving down, in case he should be cut off in the wilds of Herefordshire when he had to be on call again at the Central from midnight?

Staring out into the fairy-tale world of icicles, trees heavy with snow, sunlight catching the white-capped hills, here at home in the middle of her own family, Emily was unutterably lonely. Without James the world was empty. She'd known this, of course, since the night when she'd found him there in the Central after her belongings had been stolen, but the knowledge and certainty had been growing daily. It was James's face, tired and plain, that lived secretly in her dreams and gave meaning to her days. To have the solid comforting bulk of James alongside her, the centre of her being and the resting place for her heart, was all she asked. When he was within reach, she knew real happiness, unlike any other, and utter contentment. Excitement, too. What was more, she entertained no further worries that she might be frigid, cold, or under-sexed.

At that moment, slowly nosing its way round the bends, through the sprinkling of snow that lay undisturbed in the narrow country side roads, she glimpsed a car.

James. The Jaguar turned into the paved entrance at the side of the house, drew up alongside her father's elderly Rover.

Forgetting everything and everyone else, experiencing only the bewildering tearing delight of James's own presence, Emily ran down the stairs, through the hall, and out, coatless, into the freezing morning, to fling herself straight into his arms.

James, if she'd only known it, was as excited as she was. He'd been fighting a boyish exhilaration all along the motor-way, and his heart was thumping like any teenager's as he turned into Wistaria Lodge. Receiving Emily full pelt against his chest, he was kissed frantically on both cheeks, and before he had a chance to inhibit his response he kissed her back – not sedately on her cheek, either – and was holding her to him as he had been wanting to do for what seemed a lifetime of longing. Exhilaration swept them both, as it began to dawn on them that this could be a shared love.

All at once it became the most wonderful Christmas Emily had ever known – even if, unfortunately, it seemed to be over almost as soon as it had begun. For not only did James decide he could not, with the roads as they were, stay for dinner, but he'd hardly arrived before the traditional Boxing Day sherry party for local practitioners was under way. And Emily discovered that medicine could claim James in Wistaria Lodge just as surely as it did at the Central.

The local GPs, together with the cardiologist from the Royal Infirmary, descended on him like a rugger scrum, to ascertain what they thought at the Central about – about anything, it seemed, from the saturated fats and blood cholesterol levels to artificial valves versus homografts. Finally he and the cardiologist, Edward Langford-Thomas, held what for all practical purposes amounted to a sym-posium on heart disease at one end of the room, while the cardiologist's overpowering wife, Bossy Brenda – as she was known in every practice for miles round – attempted to ride roughshod over a group of long-suffering wives at the other. In the middle Melissa held court, various GPs and all the assistants peeling off from the cardiology symposium to refresh themselves for ten minutes or so before diving back into the medical group, where James, his shoulders propped against the bookcase, appeared to Emily to be undeniably pontificating.

'He seems to be laying down the law a bit,' she said in a startled aside to her father.

'Pundit from a top teaching hospital, after all,' he reminded her. 'Even if he does wear a distinctly with-it cheese-cloth shirt. Which I've no doubt was your Christmas present.'

Emily, to her annoyance, blushed.

Her father was pleased at the success of his shot in the dark. 'We're fortunate to capture him for our party, you know. Send my stock up locally, he will. Thanks to you, of course,' he added, gave her a noticeably sharp look. He'd seen her, that morning, from his study window, flying out to greet James. But what had shaken him out of his Boxing Day lethargy had been the sight of James greeting her. Dr Goring had gone at once in search of Valerie – who, putting finishing touches to the food, had received this latest news from the front absentmindedly.

'Em and James Leyburn?' she'd queried vaguely, her hand poised over the Quiche Lorraine she was cutting up. 'Surely not?'

'Told you she was a dish. Never thought she'd land our James, though. But it looks to me as if we may yet have a leading heart surgeon from the Central in this family.'

'Jumping to conclusions rather, aren't you?' Valerie asked, though this had never been a characteristic of his, and well she knew it.

'The lightning diagnostician, that's me,' her husband told her, picking out cashew nuts from little silver bowls and crunching them fast. 'Must say, he'll do far better with Em than with poor Melissa, silly goose. She'd never have made a doctor's wife in a thousand years.'

He repeated this opinion to his younger daughter as they stood on the sidelines for a brief respite from pushing round the food and drink.

Emily giggled cheerfully. 'Hardly,' she agreed.

'But you're different.'

'Me?' Emily opened her eyes wide and gazed innocently at him. But in their depths the lightning diagnostician recognised exactly what he had expected to find.

'Wade in and get him, Em,' he said. 'He needs someone like you.'

'I don't know –'

'Marry the bloke. I'd like another son-in-law.'

'But, Dad . . .' She was uncertain whether to be delighted or horrified.

After tea she returned to London with James, her gear in a new and incredibly expensive case which had been Melissa and Andrew's present, brought from Zürich by Andrew. At any other time she would have been overwhelmed by it, but today it registered as no more than a useful container for her possessions.

James's present to her was a thin silver chain with an aquamarine pendant, watery and fragile, swinging in a circle of silver, and now, as she sat alongside him in the Jaguar, roaring up the motorway, she fingered it tenderly. 'This is fantastic, James,' she told him. 'I'm so pleased with it.'

'I hope it's all right.' In the shop he'd thought the delicate chain with its gleaming transparent stone beautiful, its understated charm perfectly suited to Emily's small-boned loveliness. But Melissa's quick dismissive glance had unnerved him. 'I'm afraid I'm not much good at shopping for that sort of thing, though.'

Emily looked at him, recognised instantly that he was feeling his own gift diminished by that crazy great chain clanking round her sister's only too fashionable neck, seemed to be genuinely afraid he'd presented her with something not trendy enough. In the motorway lighting he had a ruddy orange glow, yet it was now for the first time that she saw him as defenceless, badly in need of her reassurance. 'I love it,' she said softly, touching his hand lightly. 'It's beautiful. And I'm not just saying that. You should know me better.'

He did, of course. Truthful. Outspoken to a fault. Though she would never knowingly hurt anyone, and he wasn't entirely sure she was being one hundred per cent straight with him now.

'I honestly am thrilled with it.' She was watching his face, as he concentrated on the road ahead, had seen the doubt flicker. 'I could never wear a great chain like that thing of Melissa's. Can you see me clanking round the hospital? It'd be a joke. Actually it is a bit of a joke already, as far as Dad's concerned. He thinks it's terrible.'

James smiled, the sudden gentle smile that so illuminated his face, a smile that already had a life of its own in Emily's memories. They sat companionably together as the Jaguar tore into London, chatted light-heartedly for a while about Wistaria Lodge, and Emily's parents, and Barnaby.

'I wonder what he'll make of Switzerland? Think of it, a chalet in Switzerland as well as the penthouse. Would you believe? But what's going to happen to poor Greg?'

'I really can't imagine,' James was unexpectedly censorious, 'what Greg and Melissa think they're playing at. A couple of irresponsible children, both of them.'

Emily was taken by surprise. A searing, tragic love affair, she'd been seeing. Or had she? Not quite, to be truthful. She understood Melissa too well now to suppose anything of the sort. 'I suppose you're right,' she admitted.

'The trouble with your sister is she's never grown up at all. She's exactly the same now as she was when I first knew her.'

'Is she?'

'A self-indulgent child. Now, by the calendar, you're years younger than she is. But in maturity years older. And you'll go on growing and developing.' Please God, she'd go on growing alongside him, for all the years ahead.

Emily was incoherent with delight. 'But, James – you can't possibly mean – after all, Melissa – she – I – there's so much I know nothing about. Melissa –'

'Oh, granted she can find her way round a few restaurants in a manner you might not achieve. Nor me, for that matter. She has a surface sophistication I'll certainly never be able to emulate.' He found this had ceased to bother him.

'S–surface sophistication?'

'No depth. She can be very misleading, of course.' He frowned, thought of his own wasted years, thrown away on an unreal dream, and all at once it came pouring out, the desert of pain and longing. All for nothing. He could never have settled down for life with Melissa. None of it had been her fault, either, he added fairly. She could no more help being the creature she was than a kitten could stop chasing its tail.

They were off the motorway now, driving through Bayswater towards St Anne's Square.

'I thought you still loved her,' Emily said in a small voice. 'Or at least . . .'

He glanced quickly at her. 'You didn't, you know.' Tonight he had all the confidence in the world, and knew exactly where he was going, and with whom. He patted her knee. 'Admit.'

'Well, no.' Emily wriggled. Her voice was even smaller. 'Not recently. But at first I did.'

'I haven't for years.'

'Years?' Marvellous. Not for years. Emily's joy so shattered her cool that she lapsed into silence while she thought this out. Not for *years*.

They were in St Anne's Square. James parked, extracted Emily's impressive new case. 'A cup of tea?' As good a way as any of keeping her with him for another hour or two.

'Yes, please.'

He put his arm round her, and together they walked up the steps to the front door.

In the kitchen they bumped around companionably, filling the kettle, putting out the cups and saucers, a tin of biscuits. Finally they sat down at the table, and Emily poured the tea, while James watched her. She was so sweet, his Em, so soft and desirable, her dark hair flopping about her cheeks so that he longed to have his hands in it. What he wanted most of all, of course, was to have her in his arms all night. Already, across the formica-topped kitchen table, he seemed to be holding her hands as though he was drowning. He was drowning. Drowning in love for Emily.

In an attempt to control his overpowering desire, he took

the aquamarine pendant, and dangled it in his fingers, turn-ing it to the light, his hands under Emily's nose.

She squinted down, pretending to herself she was looking at the aquamarine, but in reality seeing only James's hands, his fingers with their precise touch, and loving them as much as she loved every inch of him. And this, to be honest, was to the point of blind adoration. His hands were sturdy, strong, the nails cut short. She lost interest in her lovely jewellery, saw only James's hands, and knew she wanted them touching her instead of the pendant round her neck.

'Are you sure,' he was asking, still dubious, 'that you wouldn't rather have had a chunky great object like Melissa's?'

'Quite sure,' she said firmly, removing his hands from the stone and taking them into her own keeping. She held them to her lips momentarily, and then, rubbing them tenderly against her cheek, remembering what he'd said in the car during their journey, she added, on a sudden breath of con-fidence and certainty, 'Suppose we both forget all about Melissa and think about us?'

He smiled across at her, his face alive with joy. With his heart in his eyes, he leant over the table and took her small head between his two hands. 'You're so terribly young, love, are you sure you – I mean – Oh God, Em, I love you.' He took her into his arms. 'This damn table,' he muttered angrily. 'What the hell are we doing, trying to climb about over this bloody table?' He gave the offending object a great shove with his knee, so that it tilted dangerously, while their cups slid wildly. With one hand Emily righted it. But James was yelling at her. Quiet, controlled, reassuring James was bellowing. It was a wonder the windows didn't crack. But she loved it. 'To hell with the bloody table,' he was roaring. 'Leave it alone. Look at me.'

And she found herself jammed against the door of the broom cupboard. Inside it a number of objects seemed to be falling down, but James obviously didn't care, and neither did she. His heavy frame was against hers, his weight was enormous, but apparently her bones had been constructed for something like this. His body was alive against hers, while his arms held her securely. Not tenderly at all. Not any more. His lips were on hers, bruising her mouth. Sensation, excitement and love became one devouring joy, until she wanted nothing more than to be able to love James for ever.

Unexpectedly he let go of her. 'Hell,' he said, for some reason she was unable to fathom still angry. With his hands resting on the cupboard behind her he stared at her with a strange expression, his face oddly different. 'Em,' he began urgently. 'Do you want – shall we –'

The telephone rang.

James swore. 'It can bloody ring,' he said savagely.

It did, of course. It rang and rang. And with every ring James grew more uneasy, until at last he muttered 'there is this man in intensive care. I suppose I'll have to go,' and strode furiously across the passage to his bedroom.

Emily collapsed into a chair at the table, rearranged the cups automatically, and prepared to wait. Through the daze of happiness she heard his voice, questioning.

'Pulse? How does that compare . . . ? On admission? I see . . . yes . . . blood pressure? Short of breath, yes . . . what about lying down? Yes. Coughing? Phlegm? What do his lungs sound like at the bases? I see . . . no, quite. Liver?'

As he talked and listened, in a small corner of his mind another James looked at the bed, knowing that if he'd not been interrupted he'd have taken Emily there. Did he have to go across to the ward? Surely for once he was entitled to follow his own inclination, stay here with Emily?

'Right,' he said. 'I'll come over, Mark. Once I've had a look at him we can decide whether we're going to have to call the cardiologists in tonight, or whether we can hang on until the morning. Pity to call Dr Miller out on Boxing Day if we can avoid it. I'll come across stat, and we'll go over him together, and then if necessary I'll ring Dr Miller.'

Emily heard it.

No. He couldn't be going, not now, when –

'Sorry.' He came back into the kitchen. 'I'm wanted, I'm afraid. We had to admit this patient, you see, as an emergency yesterday – he was due to come in after Christmas anyway, for a new aortic valve, but it's a bit dicey. I'm not sure we're going to be able to get him fit enough for surgery – however, the main thing at the moment is to tide him over the next day or two.' He leant against the draining board in a manner already achingly familiar to her, gulping cold tea. 'If you come now, I'll see you home at the same time.'

'All right,' Emily said, feeling as if she was dying. 'Yes. Thank you, James,' she added politely, since he'd become a stranger now, remote, lost in the demands of his job. He'd forgotten she existed as a person, she was no more than a body to be moved out of his flat and into her own, while he took himself back to the Central.

Silently they went downstairs. The moment she'd thought was going to change her life had vanished, might as far as James was concerned never have happened, she was sure. His thoughts now were only for this patient in the ward, the measures that might be taken to keep him going. He was thinking about how he was going to get the man fit enough to stand surgery, so that they could give him a new valve in his heart. In short, she reminded herself sharply, to save his life. Where were her priorities?

Walking at James's side along St Anne's Square, she told herself she ought to be able to stand this sudden abrupt termination to what had been, after all, a spectacularly happy day. This was what caring for the sick meant – you couldn't choose your time and place for doing it. That was what it was all about. Her father had told her this from childhood. 'To cure sometimes, to alleviate often, to care always.' Always. Even when you didn't feel like it.

But at last she knew how you could hate the hospital that did this to you.

9. *California, Here I Come*

In the cardio-thoracic unit, of course, they spotted what had happened at once. Emily was floating round the place about three feet above ground in a state of rapt bliss, while there was no mistaking James's happiness. He kept smiling for no reason at all at no one in particular. He even, more than once, in fact, turned his radiant beam on Northiam. This startled them all, not least the Central's most eminent surgeon, seen to wince, swallow, finally produce a sickly almost ingratiating grin in return. Or so the story went, all round the department inside fifty seconds.

No one could fail to read the delight James and Emily took in one another's presence. It was as if both of them, the moment they met – or even caught sight of one another, according to report – switched on all the illuminations. James looked ten years younger, too.

Northiam and Felicity wished the pair well, and broadcast their hope that James would at last marry and settle down.

In view of this attitude, it seemed to the avid onlookers more than curious that the next invitation Northiam issued for dinner should be for James alone, and they began at once to confer, asking one another if anything could have happened to change Northiam's opinion. Had Emily, for instance, managed to upset him? Was he, after all, going to frown on the course of true love? Could he be so antiquated, out of date, prehistoric that he'd come to the conclusion that James was too senior and Emily too junior? Had he accordingly forbidden James to have an affair with Emily? If it was an affair, that is to say. This was another point fascinating everyone. How was the relationship accurately to be described?

What they were all agreed on was the extraordinary change in James. There he'd been, discharging benevolence and radiating joy. He went to dinner with Northiam one night, returned a different man. Difficult and bad-tempered in the theatre, snapping everyone's head off without provocation, morose and monosyllabic in outpatients, curt and disagreeable on ward rounds, silent at mealtimes, he'd apparently undergone some sort of personality change overnight.

What could have gone wrong? Surely James was not going to prove such a worm that he'd allow Northiam to trample over him regardless? What had James and Emily's affair to do with Northiam, in any case? All right, so the girl was working in his office. But he didn't hold the power of life and death – or even of employment and redundancy. There was a limit, surely, to the damage Northiam could inflict, even on his own staff. Of course, he'd broken careers before now, but then he couldn't afford to lose James, who was his alter ego, his second pair of hands, his stand-in. His support, too. Northiam hated depending on people, normally refused to trust anyone but himself. James, though, was different. On James Leyburn, Marcus Northiam did depend, and had done for years.

As for Emily, if Northiam chose to be difficult, she only had to transfer to another department in the hospital, and go on seeing as much as she wished of James.

One or two of the more helpful souls in the department thought it might be only kind to express this useful opinion as to her line of action to Emily herself.

She was shattered.

Until then, she had never in her wildest dreams imagined that anyone had noticed her feelings for James, far less that it could be generally apparent around the Central that she shared some sort of understanding with him. And what sort of understanding, she only wished she knew.

Her own day sprang into brilliance the moment he entered it, hope woke with her in the morning, and even the corridors of the Central had their own magic, simply because in them she and James were liable to meet at any moment and were sharing the same air – canned, flat and smelling of ether or Dettol – while round any corner she might encounter him. But James had never declared his love. He'd not only not declared it in any old-world sense, like asking for her hand in marriage – she hardly expected anything of the sort – but, to her enormous disappointment, he'd not asked for anything else either. He'd certainly failed to seize her, as she was almost sure he'd been about to do on Boxing Day in his flat, throw her down on his bed and make passionate love to her.

All that had happened was that day after day he had looked at her with naked love in his eyes. Off-duty he'd hardly been apart from her. Physically they'd been very close – but never close enough. Only their hands seemed to brush amazingly often, and he'd put what she'd known was not any longer a brotherly arm round her shoulders. He'd settle her into the Jaguar as though she were made of the most brittle spun glass – and treated her generally in fact as though he loved her and was determined to cherish her while life should last, so that although he'd failed to commit himself in words – or, alas, deed – Emily was too filled with overflowing happiness to experience a moment's alarm.

But now, as far as she could make out, people were asking her his intentions, while James had snapped off the light inside him, and suddenly the world was cold and dark.

He continued to take her out, but he was preoccupied, absent-minded, very much the irritable surgeon with too many lives in his hands, too many calls on his time, and she quickly discerned that all he asked of her now was not to put pressure on him, not to make demands, not to bother him. What she didn't know was that her presence itself relaxed him and brought a brief peace. Instead she was frightened. Was he already, so soon, bored with her, so young and naïve? He'd be far too kind to drop her abruptly, without warning.

Meanwhile, throughout this difficult period, Northiam was in high good humour, smug and pleased with himself.

They'd seen him in this mood before, when he'd pulled off some complicated surgical technique that had been baffling his colleagues. But there was nothing in the theatre to account for his present frame of mind.

And so another rumour was born. Northiam, they decided, must have taken matters into his own hands, have asked James his intentions. Cupid in person, in fact, an unlikely figure spiritually poised with his bow and arrow aimed – with his usual impeccable accuracy – at James.

Or, in another popular version then current, Northiam, the father of his family, was seeing to it that marriage was to be the outcome of this love affair. He was making sure that the youngest and newest member of the unit was not taken advantage of by the oldest and most senior. Soon there would be a Central wedding. And if it might also be described as a shotgun wedding this only added to the general excitement and sense of anticipation.

Only a tightly knit, overworked little group, of course, short of sleep and with little time for outside interests, could have evolved – and fallen for – such a load of rubbish.

Had they been fractionally more alert, they might have grasped that for someone like Northiam, who it was well known never did anything without careful planning, the move to Harley Street was the significant factor that they'd left out of their calculations. It had taken place early in the New Year. The house in St John's Wood was up for sale and most of the furniture in store, while Northiam and Felicity were installed – together, in, as far as could be observed, wedded bliss – in the Harley Street block. Exactly as James had forecast, though none of them had believed him, instead inventing far-fetched, if admittedly fascinating, possibilities.

The truth, when it came, blew all their minds.

On a cold wet day in February, Northiam summoned a departmental meeting. Medical and surgical staff were asked to assemble thirty minutes before what he presumably thought of as the other ranks, and had the news broken to them first. What James had been keeping to himself ever since that dinner in January now became apparent, and it was nothing whatever to do with shotgun weddings.

Northiam was leaving the Central London Hospital. The National Health Service, too. But not, as they'd all occasionally predicted, for private practice. Nothing so tame or ordinary.

Northiam was going to the USA.

To California, to be precise, and the Ocean Hospital. All became clear at last. This departure had been fixed up at Hampton Court, and over dinner at the Waldorf on that Monday in September. This was why Professor Cohen and Dr Flanagan had stopped off in London. Not simply to watch Northiam. To make him an offer. Which he'd accepted. Probably on the spot. What was more, he proposed, as he was now cheerfully informing the astonished assembly, to take his team along with him. 'Or such of you as may express a desire to accompany me.'

Jaws dropped, eyes consulted incredulously with others as blankly disbelieving. None of them could take the news in. Their reactions were all to pieces, and they lapsed into a recognisable state of shock.

What a tale to spread round the hospital. But what were they to do? Were they going to fly off, with cries of gladness and joy, to a new and lucrative existence in the USA? Or was the project a horrible betrayal of all they held dear, from which they could only step back in horror? Northiam, after all, was the greatest heart surgeon the Central had ever trained, some even maintained the best in the country. Were they going to have to watch him leave for an American post, remaining themselves in London in a cardio-thoracic unit that overnight would become second-rate?

This must have been the knowledge James had carried round with him for the past three weeks. Hardly surprising he'd been impossible to deal with. Now it was all in the open, what did he have to say?

His face remained stony.

Northiam however was continuing affably. He'd take up his new post in the autumn, he said. He was to be Chief of Surgery in the Cardio-Thoracic Department of the Ocean Hospital. 'There'll be none of this muddled cheese-paring economy that we're subject to here. In the Ocean Hospital I shall have adequate facilities. I'm sick and tired of trying to do good work under bad conditions. You've all seen the obstacles I've had to contend with. This used to be one of the finest teaching hospitals in the country. What is it now?' He paused, rhetorically only. None of them, in any case, were in a state to answer. 'A down-at-heel bureaucratic outpost of that run-down department at the Elephant and Castle.' He glared round. 'I don't need to tell you that a surgeon has a limited working life. I'm not going to waste mine battling with a load of memo-writing uncivil servants. Rightly or wrongly, I happen to believe I have a contribution to make towards the advancement of the surgery of the heart and blood vessels, and I propose to make it in proper surroundings.' He looked at the stunned faces. 'You're surprised,' he commented. 'I don't know why you should be. Most of you must surely have seen this coming?' They hadn't, of course. Not this. 'Think of the petty inconveniences hindering our treatment and surgery here in recent months. Far too many to enumerate.' He proceeded to enumerate in detail a number of events they all remembered extremely clearly. 'I hope I care enough about the future of heart surgery to be able to face leaving the hospital that trained me and the country I was born in, if it proves necessary for the advancement of cardio-thoracic surgery. Medicine is international, and I should hold myself to be negligent if I remained here, short-staffed, and provided with second-rate equipment, achieving only a fraction of what could be accomplished.' He glared angrily round, looked across to Felicity. 'My wife agrees with me. In the Ocean Hospital she is offered a fully equipped laboratory with a staff four times as large as she has here, most of them better-qualified too. Here, as far as we can tell, she's to be reduced next year to one man and a boy, plus a half-trained girl if she's lucky, unless she can drum up funds outside, from some charity. That's how they expect her to carry on her work. Simply not good enough. In the States we'll both be able to get down to work unimpeded by bureaucrats. In a year or two I shall be ready to inaugurate a full programme of heart transplants. No hope of that here. Not enough laboratory back-up. I hope many of you will come with me and help me launch a new phase of worthwhile, even, I think I may say, exciting work.'

Abruptly he came to the nitty-gritty. 'My wife and I are travelling out to the Ocean Hospital in the Easter vacation. By then, I should like to know which of you wish to join me there, to take up work in the autumn.' He paused, scanned their expressions. 'That's all. Any questions?'

Discussion rose to a crescendo, lasted throughout the ensuing week. The cardio-thoracic unit spent what little free time it had arguing urgently – and speculating wildly – in the corners of corridors, or in the King's Head, planning its future in the USA.

The hospital was as shaken as the unit. As he'd done throughout his professional life, Northiam came in for a great deal of criticism. But there was approval, too, as well as a sense of fatalism. 'This is what we've come to,' people told one another. 'This is what the administration has brought us to.' Dinners, lunches, cups of tea or coffee, glasses of alcohol or tomato juice were consumed up and down Harley Street, in half a dozen clubs, after outpatients, in common rooms and bars, offices and laboratories, while lists and appointments were disrupted by the number of senior consultants who suddenly took to using the stairs instead of the lifts. 'We'll just have a word on the way down' – to be discovered, half an hour or more later, by distraught housemen or semi-hysterical secretaries arguing on the first landing.

Though they asserted they were well aware they were doomed to failure – 'Northiam's always been immovable once he's made up his mind, but I felt I owed it to the hospital at least to try' – a great many people made the attempt to persuade him to stay on at the Central.

But Northiam was going to California, and with him, it soon appeared, he'd be taking not only his medical and surgical team, anaesthetists, pathologists, immunologists, radiologists, physiologists, but sisters from the cardio-thoracic theatre, intensive care and the wards, as well as theatre and laboratory technicians.

Quite a group were to accompany Northiam and Felicity

on their preliminary visit to California in April. Apparently the Ocean Hospital, elated to have landed Northiam, were prepared to pay fares for an army of his supporters to case the joint. The cardio-thoracic unit would be working at half-strength during his absence – he normally took three weeks holiday in the Easter vacation, and it was customary, during this period, for James, with what amounted to the second eleven, to carry out the routine cold surgery, while unit holidays were fitted in during the great man's absence. Wendy Stourbridge was to go with Northiam to see to the paperwork, one of the senior sisters from intensive care went along too, and a consultant anaesthetist flew out for seven days, together with two senior registrars.

By this time Northiam had appeared on television and radio, on news bulletins and discussion programmes. He'd explained with acerbity and precision exactly what was lacking in the facilities available to heart surgeons under the Health Service in Great Britain. Spokesmen for the Department of Health had been forced to appear the following days to point out how mistaken he was. Their arguments were countered by others, from the Royal Colleges, other hospitals and medical schools, some of them doing their best to pour oil on troubled waters and reassure everyone all round, others maintaining that there was a lot in what Northiam said, and if the Americans could give him proper facilities he'd need his head examining if he didn't go.

At the Central they were, predictably, furious. Northiam had always been a damn nuisance. Unfortunately, he also happened to be easily their most illustrious son, and if he left the country the hospital's famous cardio-thoracic department would have sunk without trace. This could not be allowed, at any price. They redoubled their efforts to make him abandon his plan, even succeeding in extracting promises of improved facilities, and an improved budget, with a special subsidy from one of the medical foundations. To no effect. Reluctantly, they pulled themselves together and began to search for a replacement. The post was advertised – glowingly – and feelers were thrown out to heart surgeons up and down the country.

At Easter, Northiam and his by now heavily swollen entourage took off for California. James was left in charge of the department and Emily of the office. But she hardly saw him. If he came in, she'd be on the telephone, or typing tapes wildly, trying to catch up. He'd collect the letters she'd typed, which were awaiting signature, and carry them off with him to sign during outpatients. Afterwards his houseman or one of the nurses would bring them back. Emily would sort them out, put them into their envelopes, occasionally catch a glimpse of him in the corridor as she galloped along to catch the post. When she returned, the room would be empty. There'd be a hasty note on her desk, and another collection of tapes.

Their time together was over, gone, part of the past, she told herself, and she must accept it. As soon as he'd been confronted with this rush of work, coupled with the heavy responsibilities he carried in Northiam's absence, she'd slipped from his mind. It was only to be expected, she reminded herself fairly. She found it unbearable.

For now they had no future together. She was going to be left behind in the Central, this was clear. Northiam certainly wasn't going to need her in his new life.

10. A Smooth Operator

At this point Northiam took a hand, resuming his role as the most improbable Cupid the Central had ever known. He was motivated, needless to say, by self-interest.

In California he remarked to Wendy Stourbridge, one morning at breakfast in the hotel where they were all staying, 'Of course, I know there's no hope of persuading that husband of yours to uproot himself from London, so I don't suppose I can expect you to come out here permanently and run my office, eh?'

Wendy confirmed that she had no intention of breaking up her marriage and moving to California in order to maintain continuity in office routines.

'No, well, wish you would, but there it is. If you won't, you won't. Now, what about that nice little soul Emily? Do you think she'd come out? Useful if she did.'

'Well, I . . .'

'Don't want some strange American girl. Need someone who understands my methods, knows my routine. If Emily came out here, the system you and I worked out together could continue. Emily's a sensible, methodical child. I'd know where I stood.'

Wendy regarded him cautiously. She had a strong suspicion he was up to something.

His next sentence confirmed this impression.

'James gets on with Emily.' Northiam twinkled benevolently. 'In fact he's rather smitten with her if you ask me.' It was, of course, the last thing anyone would consider asking him. 'Something in the wind, I shouldn't wonder. Like to see old James settling down.' He stared agreeably at Wendy over his coffee cup, benign and limpid-eyed, as though his life was spent in arranging suitable matches for the dear young people on his staff. 'Don't you think it would be nice for James to have Emily out here?'

Wendy, for once, was rattled. 'Er – I – yes, I suppose so. But – um – what about the cost? Who would pay her fare? I don't really think it likely the hospital would be prepared to finance that, do you?'

'See no reason why they shouldn't.'

Northiam, as usual, proved to be correct. The Ocean Hospital, delighted to have landed Northiam, the biggest fish in its sea, was ready to pay fares for any number of his staff, the little girl in the office – as he persisted in referring to her – equally with the surgeons, physicians and anaesthetists in his team.

And so Emily's spirits sky-rocketed when, in the first spare minutes they had on the hectic day of Northiam's return to the Central, Wendy told her of the plans for her to move to the Ocean Hospital as Northiam's personal secretary, to run his office there.

'Me? You don't mean it?' She could hardly contain her exuberance. It ran away with her, sparked out all round the room, bouncing off filing cabinets and desks. 'But – but – '

'Of course,' Wendy felt obliged to remind her, 'you are very inexperienced. But you will have had a year with him by September, and as I can't leave London, he'd like you to go with him. He doesn't want new people around him.'

He wasn't, it soon became clear, going to have new people. Hardly anyone on his staff was remaining at the Central, and work in the cardio-thoracic unit had been resumed at top pressure. There seemed no end to the consultations and surgery that had somehow to be fitted in before Northiam's departure, while in addition, the advertisements having appeared in the medical press during his absence in California, there were the applicants for the post of his successor to be interviewed, together with huge numbers of applicants from potential replacement staff.

The dean of the medical school, who was good at this sort

of thing, had taken it on himself to heal the breach between the Central's administration and its departing heart surgeon, and as a result Northiam was to vet the applicants himself and to sit on the selection committee.

While all this was going on, Emily had little opportunity to talk to James about California. He was up to his eyebrows in work and seemed, as far as she could tell, to live entirely in the present, literally almost moment to moment. With each packed day holding so many demands, to look forward to another life in another country was self-indulgence. But Emily no longer worried. Thanks to Northiam's invitation, she could again count on a future shared with James. No need, after all, to face the prospect of losing him at the end of the summer. Long days, weeks, months stretched gloriously ahead, under blue skies and Californian sun.

She came down to earth with a bump. One evening they'd been booked for a rare meal together, but were having a drink in James's flat, still at the stage of discussing where they should eat, when the telephone summoned him. After a detailed conversation, he put it down and apologised. 'I'll have to go. God knows how long I'll be – I don't like the sound of it. Hell, I did particularly want to talk to you tonight.'

'I'll hang around.' She was easy, unsuspecting – if anything, pleased. It was weeks since they'd talked properly – or improperly, which was what she was longing for, of course.

He sighed. 'I'm sorry, Em. Look –'

'Supposing I wait here for half an hour, and you give me a ring when you've some idea how long you'll be.'

'Right.'

He'd rung and said he'd be another hour, and she'd better eat, so she'd gone home to the attic flat and made herself bacon and eggs. He'd turned up there at ten o'clock, offering to take her for a drink. She'd refused, had cooked more bacon and eggs and made coffee. He'd eaten voraciously, and then, over the coffee, sitting with his mug in his hands on her divan, frowning, dwarfing the little room so that suddenly it seemed too small and prettified for anyone but a child, he told her that he was putting in for Northiam's post.

The walls closed in on Emily, the room threatened to stifle her, and she experienced an acute sense of revulsion for its cosy charm. Never again would she feel the same about her bedsitting room in Barbie Henderson's flat – in those two or three seconds of catastrophic reassessment she went right off it.

James was talking about his future plans. His, not hers. 'Northiam's post? You?' Emily's hand shook, and before she lost all control and spilt it everywhere, she put her coffee mug down carefully on the rush matting.

'Yes. I shan't get it, but I'm putting in for it.'

This briefly diverted her. 'Of course you'll get it,' she said robustly. 'But – '

But, she was asking herself, why hadn't he told her this before? If he had, she would never have thought of going to California. Others in the unit, too, had they known James proposed to remain at the Central, might have been less eager to leave.

This was why he'd said nothing, of course. He explained it to her in detail. What it came down to was that he had promised at the outset not to queer Northiam's pitch. Being James, he had kept his word, no matter what tricks Northiam got up to. 'No good swinging about like a Yo-yo at every twitch on the string from that old devil. Make up your mind and stick to it, that's how to deal with him. It's the only way. Of course, he still wants me to go with him. He hasn't for a minute accepted my decision to stay in London. He keeps on at me about it daily, blast him.' He smiled, wearily but humorously. To be on the winning side, to have Northiam, whatever he might pretend, the suppliant, had been a change, and it had given him a more tolerant, even a wryly affectionate attitude to his bloody-minded chief.

'Oh James, if only you'd told me. I'd never have said I'd – '

'No, well, of course it was a bit of a shock when I heard about that. But I've been thinking about it, and – '

'Of course I shan't go.'

'That's what I wanted to talk to you about. You must go with him, you know. It'll be superb experience for you, and you can't throw it away on my account, to hang around in

London with me. That would never do. I'd never forgive myself.'

'But, James, don't you see – ?'

They'd argued until they were both exhausted and miserable. Emily had even wept. James comforted her, but remained adamant. He'd thought this out, and he was certain she must not give up the Californian post. 'Go for a year, at least.'

Finally they'd separated. James was plainly dropping on his feet, and it was Emily who ceased the fruitless argument. They were getting nowhere, and James looked so worn and unhappy she could stand it no longer. But as soon as he'd gone she felt worse than ever, and walked about the tiny hated room arguing the problem through time after time. James was wrong. She was certain of it. For once he was totally wrong. It might sound a splendid idea to go to California for a year, and run Northiam's office, be his personal secretary at the Ocean Hospital. Of course, career-wise it was promotion. And, as James had pointed out, if she took it on for only a year, when she returned to the Central they'd offer her a much better post as a result. Much more senior than the junior position she had now. Moreover, she had to admit, even in the midst of her misery, she'd enjoy it. But it was basically wrong. The priorities were wrong. What counted was the love she and James shared, and this was what should come first. She spent an unhappy night, hardly slept at all, went heavy-eyed to the office and confided in no one. What could she say? She was caught in a trap she'd sprung herself. She could hardly waltz airily in this morning, announce she'd decided overnight not to go to California, thank you. 'Blow you, Marcus Northiam, I'm staying here in London with my bloke James.' And then James would deny it, in any case.

She'd have to wait, take her time, say nothing. She must talk to James again, thrash it all out with him. Until then, she must keep silence. There were months in hand, fortunately. Four months, to be precise. No need to make a decision or to tell Northiam anything at all, for at least four weeks. That would be plenty of time.

Head down, tight-lipped and furious, she banged the type-writer grimly, and snapped down the telephone.

Everyone, of course, knew exactly why. Round her the department was rocking. The news that James had put in for Northiam's post produced almost as many shock waves in the Central as Northiam's original decision to leave for the States.

Only two people kept their heads when the news broke. One was James himself, who went on saying nothing, as he'd been doing since January. The other was Northiam. Both of them, of course, were hardly taken by surprise, and North-iam now admitted he'd known James's intentions from the beginning and had done his best, as he confided widely, to put a stop to what he chose to refer to as 'Leyburn's mis-guided attempt to take my place here.'

Mark Corrie, when he heard this, made a chopping motion with his hand, while his companions nodded.

It became increasingly clear that only over Northiam's dead body would James Leyburn succeed him. And since Northiam was very much alive and showed every sign of remaining in excellent health, not to mention vigorous activity, the outlook for James's appointment to the post of director of the cardio-thoracic unit was distinctly poor.

Circumstances, too, played into Northiam's hands (they often did, and no one had ever been able to decide whether this was because he was amazingly lucky, or whether it was the result of earlier unobtrusive manipulation of events). In this case the circumstances, everyone agreed, might have been foreseen, and had no doubt been discerned on the hori-zon by Northiam long before anyone else had thought of making a reconnaissance.

Tom Rennison put in for the post. He had always been outstanding, and was, as Northiam informed everyone with piercing clarity, the inevitable first choice.

The fact could not be denied. And so the Central had hardly recovered from the shock of finding that James had put in for his chief's job before they began to pass the word round that he'd been regrettably ill-advised to do so. 'Poor old James, he hasn't a hope,' they told one another, wagging sad admonitory heads. 'With Rennison in the field he's had it.'

'Rennison should never have been allowed to leave here in the first place.'

'For God's sake, the man went to prison.'

'I know there were problems.'

'He was off the register for a year at least.'

'I suppose he must have been. But times have changed – nowadays he'd surely have got away with a fine, don't you think? Possibly a suspended sentence. And he'd never have left here.'

'At one point we certainly imagined he'd be back inside two years, at the outside – but Northiam suddenly ratted on him, if you remember.'

'I remember all right. And Leyburn got the job. But he must have known at the time he only landed it because Rennison wasn't available?'

'He knew it then. But he may have forgotten by now. After all, he is very good, there's no doubt of that, and I daresay he assumes that after all this time working with Northiam he's improved out of all recognition, while Rennison might have been expected to stand still after he left here.'

'Certainly James has improved immensely. In his own way he's very good indeed. And gets good results. But Tom left everyone standing – and he hasn't been marking time, either. He's been with Bidmead at Queen Alexandra's – Assistant Director of the Paediatric Heart Unit there.'

Wendy Stourbridge heard the talk and decided she ought to pass it on to Emily. Wendy had eyes in her head – like everyone at the Central, sticking out on stalks most of the time – and she knew Emily was going to be upset. Better for her to hear these dismal forecasts in the comparative privacy of the office than, unprepared, meet the comments flying around in the canteen, or receive the news in Northiam's own eagle-eyed presence.

Emily flinched. 'You mean James won't *get* the post?' This had never occurred to her. All right, so the light in her own world had gone out when she knew James was not going to California. But that he might not be given the post, that someone else might snatch it from him, had not crossed her mind. Who was this Tom Rennison? She was swept first with anger, then with an agonising pity, but above all, of course, with love – a love that for the first time began to verge on the maternal. It was only hours later that a flicker of feeling she tried to suppress came too. Hope. Did this mean that James would after all be coming to California?

Certainly this was what Northiam intended, as Wendy saw clearly. 'I knew he was up to something when he arranged for Emily to go to the Ocean Hospital,' she said furiously to her husband. 'I thought at first it was simply that he was looking after No. 1 as usual, but I had an intuition that there was more to it than that. And of course I was right.'

Her husband nodded. 'The crafty old bastard is always several steps ahead of everyone else. He didn't intend James to get the job – probably counted on Tom putting in for it – and he was neatly placing an added inducement in California ready for the day when James had to swallow his pride and go out there with him, whatever he might have said. In the meantime, the old so-and-so had made sure of a good secretary, already trained in his ways.'

'I suppose he must have known Tom would put in, when you come to think about it.'

'Probably wrote off and instructed him to.'

'Do you honestly think – ? If so, he did it in his own abominable scrawl. Nothing went through the office.'

'He's not that simple, dear.'

'He's not simple at all. He's the most devious man I've ever come across. If Tom Rennison is going to be appointed, I must say it'll be a pleasant change to work for someone straightforward like him, instead of for the equivalent of some Byzantine emperor at his most underhand.'

The talk continued, speculation increased, bets were laid. Some people even asserted scouts had been permanently placed at strategic points to spot Tom Rennison's approach from the outskirts of Greater London for a preliminary visit to the unit, before the official interviews took place. Others pointed out that this would be wasted effort. Tom Rennison only had to put his toe over the threshold for the information to be carried instantly to theatres, laboratories, wards and outpatients. No amount of bureaucracy or economy cuts had ever been known to impair the speed and accuracy of the Central's grapevine, which functioned today as efficiently as always.

The only human being apparently untouched by all this gossip and speculation was James. He lived in the still, quiet centre of the storm. No one dared to ask him what he thought, how he felt, what he imagined his chances to be. And even if they had dared, there was hardly an opportunity. He was working flat out, and was only to be caught on the hoof, as he passed from theatre to intensive care to outpatients, calling in occasionally – though more often Mark Corrie came instead – to deliver new tapes, sign his letters, deal with the accumulation of messages, answer queries. Emily saw so little of him that she lived for the few minutes he did spend in the office, but too often on these occasions the telephone rang, and while she answered it, James spoke hastily to Wendy, and began on his letters. When she came off the line, he'd have finished signing them, and she'd tear off to catch the post. On her return he'd have gone, the only reminder of his presence the tapes. She found the familiar voice on the reels comforting, to tell the truth. But no substitute for James himself.

11. The Farewell Party

From his window James saw her go by. He'd been going to ring her, had the telephone in his hand, to ask her if she'd like to go out for a meal. He opened the window to call out to her – but stopped. She was on her way, he realised, to some sort of party with those drop-outs at the end of the square – carrying a bottle of wine, slim and beautiful in her long Indian cotton skirt with a silky black top. The thought of the crowd he'd encounter in the basement at No. 4 made him pause – and she turned the corner. In the nightmare hours that followed, he was to curse himself for that momentary hesitation. If only he'd followed his instinct, she'd have been safe. Instead, fatally, he let her go. He'd stroll along there himself in an hour or two, he decided, collect her, and take her off for what remained of the evening.

Only an accidental meeting with Carmel, whom she'd run into in the canteen, had taken Emily along to No. 4. The council were closing down the hostel, Carmel told her. Everyone was leaving, and there was to be a farewell party that evening. A little nostalgically, Emily had decided she'd drop in, say goodbye to them all.

From the beginning, though, she wished she hadn't come. As far as she was concerned, the party was a disaster. For one thing, it was the first time in months she'd been out in the evening without James. She missed him quite abominably, and as a result found the students more than usually irritating. Either they wanted to make love to her – instantly, as far as she could tell, dodging the lean denimed bodies that surged wildly round her – or expected her to listen sympathetically to their despairing tales of the outrageous council, breaking up for reasons of pettifogging

134

economy a group making a unique contribution to the understanding of the disturbed and deprived urban delinquent. Emily stifled a yawn, agreed the contribution was unique – though by this she didn't exactly mean what they did – drank Coke out of a mug labelled Julian, and wondered what had happened to the bottle of Yugoslav Riesling she had brought with her.

Where had all the magic gone? Tonight the basement was nothing more than a low-ceilinged, noisy room, stuffy and barren of any sort of charm, filled with a crowd of rowdy students getting drunk. Wanting James, longing only to escape, she thought she'd see Susan and William and then leave. Better an evening in the flat on her own than in this dump.

She found Susan, and asked about Greg – she worried about him, felt, however ridiculously, half responsible for Melissa's abandonment of him, trading him in for a Swiss chalet.

He had already left for his grammar school in Somerset, Susan told her.

'Is he getting on all right, do you know?'

Susan shrugged. Tired and drawn, she hadn't bothered to change out of her jeans. Her nails were broken, her hands engrained with grime. 'William thinks he'll be OK in the long run,' she said. 'And working in this grammar school should suit him much better than trying to cope here. Once he's settled in he should cheer up. But it's bound to take a bit of time before he gets over your sister.'

Somewhere in Somerset, Emily thought, Greg was suffering. As for what Melissa might be feeling, who could say? But she and Greg had been so happy, so much in love. While it lasted, their love had been genuine. Emily remembered the quiet loving voices and the uninhibited joy she'd overheard. Now all that was over, finished. She searched for a meaning, experienced only a sad sense of loss. Greg's loss. Andrew and Barnaby's gain.

Susan collapsed on the basement stairs behind her. 'Oh God,' she said. 'I'm so bloody tired.' She pushed her unkempt blonde hair back and began to unburden herself. 'I know it sounds heartless, but I was thankful to see the back of Greg. He was nothing but a nuisance towards the end.'

Emily sat down on the stairs beside her. 'In what way?'

'Over this place, mainly. You know it was all his idea, using this house as sleeping quarters, and he somehow managed to sell the proposition to the council? Well, in the end things got completely out of hand, and we honestly hadn't the faintest idea who was sleeping here, or why. It was just a sort of doss house.'

Emily could believe it.

'You know the students used to smoke pot, too?'

Emily nodded.

'Of course the next step was they were on to acid, upstairs in the big dormitory. One night someone had a bad trip and nearly killed himself trying to fly out of the window. It's over the area — well, you know — and there must be at least a twenty-foot drop. If he'd gone through he'd have broken his skull and probably his spine too, William said — if he hadn't impaled himself on the railings first of all. Fortunately, though, the others managed to haul him back in and sit on him. After that, William read the riot act generally and threw out half of them.'

'Good for him.'

'I've never seen him so angry. But he went on worrying about this place, and eventually he went to the council, and told them he wasn't happy about it being used and he'd like it surveyed.'

'Surveyed?' Emily goggled. 'Surely any surveyor would condemn it on the spot?'

'That's what William thought. In fact, though, nothing happened for weeks and weeks — you know what the council are. Then when a surveyor did finally show up, he nearly had a fit.'

Emily had to laugh. 'Can you wonder?' she asked.

'Quite soon after that, a positive army of surveyors and architects and engineers, from the Greater London Council and the Ministry as well as the local council, plus a crowd of health inspectors and gas board engineers and Uncle Tom Cobley and all descended on the entire terrace and marched through every single house in force, all writing away like mad in their notebooks. So now they've decided the whole terrace must come down. They say it's unsafe and can't be repaired. The demolition men and the bulldozers are moving in.'

'When?'

'Next month. It was to have been this month, but William persuaded them to postpone it because of the difficulty of placing the children. Most of them have gone now, though, we've only half a dozen left. Of course they're the real problem kids, the ones no one would have at any price, but even they go on Monday.' She sighed, leant back against the greasy, soot-laden wall. 'Eighteen months we'll have been here. Sometimes it seems more like eighteen years. We were so hopeful when we came, we honestly thought we'd be able to build the hostel up into something worthwhile, some sort of pattern for future care. If we'd had enough staff perhaps we might have managed it. But we hadn't. Just William, Greg and me, and thirty kids. Thirty rip-roaring disturbed delinquent kids. And Greg mooned about thinking of Melissa, the students came and went to suit themselves, and a load of layabouts came for the free bed and didn't give a damn about anyone. And then we had Matthew, writing his thesis, all doctrine and no practical experience. Not that I'm not very fond of Matthew. At least he stuck it out, and he was always the same.'

'He doesn't seem to be here tonight.'

'No, he's gone off in the van to his new pad. He's got some new mates somewhere in Islington, in a squat. Not so convenient for the LSE, but they've a garden and they're going to grow vegetables. He seems to think – '

A long-haired, bearded student broke in. 'Sue, William wants you – the soonest. He is missing two kids, Joe and Nathan.'

'Oh, my God. Those two. Right, I'm on my way. See you, Em, some place, some time.' She dived into the smoke-filled basement.

Emily had had enough. More than enough, in fact. Unnoticeably, she stepped backwards, up the basement stairs where Susan had been sitting, until she reached the hall above. The roar of the party came up from below, and in one way she wanted nothing more than to fade quietly out of the scene. But this was the last time she'd stand in this hall, and her mind inevitably went back to that first morning in September, when she'd stood here alone and uncertain, a stranger to London, and James, incredibly, no more than Melissa's friend.

Before she left the house to the bulldozers and the demolition men, she'd have one final glance into her attic room – the room, where, after all, her London life had begun, the room which had marked the beginning of her independence. She'd look across the square once more to James's flat and remember how she'd stared across and seen it on those cold early mornings.

She climbed the four flights for the last time. The little room with its sloping ceiling gaped blankly at her, and said nothing, either of the past or the future. It seemed dead and empty, forlorn and without personality. The paint was peeling, and the damp seeped into her bones, even on this summer's evening. Surely she couldn't have lived here?

Slowly she came downstairs again, knowing that she had left this part of her life behind for ever.

The door to the big L-shaped room on the first floor, with its graceful balconied windows, stood wide, and she walked in. Camp beds and inflatable mattresses were scattered about it at individualistic angles, and she picked her way through the miscellaneous gear – mugs, cases, tote bags, sandals, boots, tights drying on a line strung across the window, cornflakes, someone's ancient typewriter and a pile of sociology textbooks – to the tall windows, open to the soft evening air, and looked out into the square.

To her delight, she saw James approaching. He must somehow have guessed where she was and be on his way to join her. She waved enthusiastically.

He waved cheerfully back, while she made signs to him to wait for her outside the house, she was on her way down. He nodded vigorously, and, filled with the utter content his presence brought, she turned away from the window, crossed the room to go to the door.

What was that?

Mice? Or a rat?

Or a human being?

Perhaps the missing children, Jo and – what was the other one called?

Emily turned back, went round the corner and found herself confronting, just as she'd expected, two of the children from next door.

'What do you two think you're doing in here?'

The answer, of course, was obvious. They were going through the scattered belongings, looking for something to sell.

They were young, quite small – not much higher than her waist. The next step, she decided, was obviously to escort them back to Susan and William, who were no doubt hunting for them. First of all, though, they had better replace whatever they had stolen.

That these two ten-year-olds might be dangerous never entered her head.

It should have done. For these disturbed children were unpredictable at the best of times, and for them this was the worst of times. On Monday they were to be sent away from the only home they knew, and separated from Susan, whom they had almost begun to love.

They backed away from Emily first, but then, cornered and alarmed, since she was between them and the door, decided to rush her.

They came hurtling at her. And she saw the open flick knife.

'Don't be ridiculous,' she said sharply. So far the situation struck her as no more than that. She didn't for a second suppose the child intended to use the knife, he was posturing, indulging in some melodramatic threat, an adventurous pretence, that was all.

His companion appeared to agree with her. 'Don't be daft, Jo,' he screeched. 'You can't use that.'

'You mind yours,' Jo retorted, and thudded into Emily.

The force of his impact carried them both on to the

balcony. She called out to James, while at the same moment she grabbed Jo's knife arm, forced it upwards and away from them both, and twisted, trying to make him drop the knife.

But the second child came racing to his aid. 'Let my mate go,' he screamed, slamming into her, kicking and flailing. Jo, excited by his support, frenzied almost, lunged upwards with the knife.

The bright blood spurted.

The two children, suddenly silenced, stared, backed off the balcony and were lost in the room behind them.

Emily started to follow them. Or this was what she intended, but she found herself falling – was she dropping to her knees, or was the balcony crumbling beneath her?

There seemed to be a lot of blood, too. Could it be hers?

It must be.

12. Emily

From Casualty, Emily went direct to the cardio-thoracic suite, the senior registrar in anaesthetics on one side, and James, walking like an old, old man, on the other.

In the Central they were already saying that if James had not been there on the spot Emily might not have survived to reach the hospital. He'd saved her life, so the story went, there on the pavement in St Anne's Square, had travelled with her in the ambulance, seen her into Casualty, and rung Northiam. He arrived from Harley Street within minutes, heard James's account of Emily's injuries.

'Lucky you were there,' he commented. 'A stab wound – a child with a flick knife? Disgraceful. Striking upwards? I see. So you think it has penetrated not only the pleural space but right through into the lung? Very probable.' Emily's lung, in fact, had collapsed, and there was now loose air in her chest that had escaped into it from her own lung. This air, together with the blood caused by the knife wound, was filling the space between her rib cage and her lung, and preventing the lung from expanding again, so that she could use it to breathe normally.

'I think the first step is to have a look inside with a thorascope to see if she's still bleeding, don't you?' As usual, he didn't in fact expect an answer. 'Yes, and then if she is, we can control it – by diathermy, say. Only a quick anaesthetic, then, Peter – we shouldn't need to open up the chest, or go in for any major surgery. Nothing like that seems likely to be called for. No.' For Northiam this was no more than minor, even trivial, routine, but it was his skill in these basic techniques that had built his reputation in the early days.

His brilliance had ceased to surprise them. But this evening he was to succeed in startling them all.

'Jamie, boy,' he said suddenly, looking up as he was fiddling with the thorascope, 'you look done in y'self.'

Since James had looked done in long before the end of Northiam's list on countless occasions, everyone stared incredulously, while Mark Currie rolled the syllables silently round his palate like vintage claret, savouring each word, treasuring it to relate the astonishing remark verbatim round the unit.

Northiam, though, had hardly begun. 'Use a stool – take the weight off your feet. You don't look too good, m'boy.' This from Northiam of all people, who for years past had never shown any sign whatsoever of grasping the elementary fact that his staff owned feet, let alone bodies to weigh on these appendages. 'Mark and I can manage very nicely on our own, I daresay. Eh?'

His bewildered juniors were too busy gaping at Northiam himself to notice what he'd spotted with only a fraction of his attention.

There was something very wrong with James. At Northiam's suggestion, he dragged a stool forward, a little clumsily, and sat there, grimly, lips compressed, eyes narrowed.

Northiam looked over at him.

'Not to worry, laddie,' he said, in a gentle voice he ordinarily used only to severely ill patients. 'The only real danger would have been in not getting her in time. All quite straightforward now, I feel sure of it.'

He was right, of course.

'Yes, well, that's very satisfactory, isn't it?' he said finally. 'No more bleeding. Now we can wash the blood out of the pleural space, and I should say, provided there's no further air leak, we can expect that lung to be coming up nicely again inside a week. In the meantime, I think, don't you, that . . . ' He began discussing with the anaesthetist and Mark Corrie the immediate measures to be taken, and was told about the bed that had been arranged for Emily in the ward. 'Right, you can get her along there now, and get a drip going. She may be a bit shocked. At least a pint of blood in the pleural space, wasn't there? And she'd lost — what would you say? I'd estimate another pint myself, before she came in.'

The voices went on, but James was losing touch with them. He stood up slowly, carefully, and made for the corridor.

Out of the corner of his eye, Northiam glimpsed the departing back. He nodded to Mark. 'Go after him,' he said crisply, and went on talking to the anaesthetist.

In the passage outside, the floor was coming up to meet James. He sat down fast, intending to put his head between his knees, but as he leant forward, such a wave of pain swept across him that he grunted aloud, and the world swam out of focus.

Mark halted just in time to avoid falling headlong over him, and bent down. Distantly, James observed his blurred image floating in the air before the clouds closed in. 'Hurt my back when she fell,' he told the head faintly.

Mark just caught the attenuated whisper. James's colour — his skin looked like cold porridge — told him more.

James came round to find Northiam eyeing him narrowly. Nothing unusual about this. It had been going on for years. But what was distinctly odd was that on this occasion he appeared to be upside down. Peculiar, that. In fact, he never remembered it happening before. He frowned, puzzled, and became aware of a number of feet ranged round his eye level. Even odder.

Northiam bent down, took his wrist. 'You're in pain,' he informed James accusingly.

As if he needed telling.

He'd had two or three seconds warning before the rusted railings of the balcony gave way, and it had been just enough. As soon as Emily appeared there above him, fighting off the children, as it appeared, he'd doubted whether the ironwork would hold if they crashed into it, and as she came down he was ready for her, spreadeagled against the area railing, his feet wedged on the lintel of the kitchen door. He'd caught her all right, prevented her from crashing down into the paved area beneath. His arms had held her securely, but the force of well over a hundred pounds of Emily landing on him from more than ten feet up had not only knocked him breathless and bruised him badly as he'd been thrust hard against the railing, but had, it turned out, fractured two of his ribs.

They examined him, X-rayed him and put him to bed under sedation in a convenient side ward Northiam had drummed up from nowhere. Since James had intended to spend the night hovering over Emily in the ward, making sure she was all right, he argued strenuously against this programme. But he was exhausted, and they'd drugged him too, so without realising it he drifted into an uneasy and highly quarrelsome series of dreams, in which he found himself constantly addressing astonishing remarks to various individuals, all of whom finally melted into a dictatorial Northiam, poised improbably on his head.

In the morning, he extracted himself stiffly from sheets and pillows, succeeded – very slowly, and gasping as pain hit him – in dressing, and finally made his appearance in the corridor, to the staff nurse's alarm and consternation. 'But, Mr Leyburn, Mr Northiam distinctly said he'd be coming in himself to look at you, and until then you weren't even – what am I going to *tell* him?' The despairing wail pursued him as he departed doggedly, if a trifle unsteadily and at a snail's pace, in the direction of the women's ward, determined to check on Emily for himself. He'd intended to spend the night at her side – and here he was, turning up at breakfast time.

'I know, laddie.' Northiam was already there, and in his parental, caring role, it seemed. 'But in fact she's been under sedation, and she's hardly had an opportunity to notice your absence. Going on nicely, too.' He passed Emily's notes, which he'd been considering when James arrived, over to him. 'She'll do,' he said. 'Nothing to worry about now. You got to her in time. Done more damage to yourself, I shouldn't wonder. However . . . ' He paused, looked James up and down. 'You stay here and keep an eye on her, eh? I'll ask sister to get hold of a comfortable chair and you can spend the day here.'

And so, when Charles Goring arrived, he found James settled in the chair by Emily's side.

Emily herself was conscious, and apparently pleased to see her father, though she informed him there was no need to leave the practice on her account. 'I'm all right now, and anyway James is here.' That, apparently, was the end of it.

For most of the next twenty-four hours James remained with Emily. By the united efforts of the Resident Surgical Officer, Mark Corrie, sister and the staff nurse – not to mention Charles Goring, who went with him – he was persuaded to go off for a meal in the early afternoon.

'He seems to be specialling her himself,' sister remarked with an indulgent smile. 'Aren't they sweet together? Isn't she a lucky girl?'

Mark Corrie, who was in sister's office, looked across through the glass partitions, towards Emily and James. He'd had a difficult day with Northiam. 'Jamie, boy,' he repeated a little sarcastically, in imitation of his unloved chief. 'Well, I suppose he can rest there as well as anywhere else.'

In spite of his ribs, James was on duty again before the week was out. The rush of work went on. He managed, though, to see Emily in every spare moment, and in the ward, where they'd always relied on his support, a new attitude was born. They took over, too, the new nickname Jamie boy, which had raced round the hospital like a prairie fire within seconds of its utterance by Northiam. A stranger coming into the cardio-thoracic department might well have supposed, from the way the sisters, nurses and orderlies behaved, that Jamie boy was a five-year-old in need of care and protection, given to them for fostering, Northiam's own battered baby, instead of a hefty six foot surgeon with two fractured ribs. They took over responsibility, as far as could be seen, for his diet, his laundry and his general wellbeing, including the management of his personal relationships.

Except for a certain mild irritation at the ceaseless flow of undesired beverages – tea, coffee, Horlicks, Ovaltine,

Bengers, Complan and even Lucozade were constantly thrust at him from every quarter – James was unconscious of their loving concern. He had no eyes for them – as they were well aware – only for Emily. And she, naturally, saw no one but him.

In fact she zipped through her recovery at a rate of knots, either gazing happily at James or dreaming quietly about him. No anxiety. James was here. She had nothing to worry about, she was going to be all right. James said so. Obediently she swallowed whatever they gave her, took deep and painful breaths as ordered by the physiotherapist, crept wobbling out of bed and sat in a chair, tottered up and down the passage, took more deep breaths and coughed, however excruciating this was, as ordered. She was a model patient, who gave no one any trouble at all, and within two weeks – though it seemed to her more like two months – she was discharged, and James drove her down to Wistaria Lodge.

Northiam, maintaining his paternal role, saw them off almost as tenderly as his ward sister. 'James will look after you,' he announced unnecessarily, as though this might have remained undiscovered, without his communication. 'Go home and get well. I've spoken to y'father and he understands y'condition. Central man, in any case. The country will do you good, too. Plenty of fresh air, exercise, eh? I want to see you fit and restored to me, ready to leave for California in September, don't forget.'

Though its intended recipient hardly noticed this injunction, sister registered it, duly broadcast the implications. 'He's got it all sewn up,' she told her staff nurse on her return to the ward.

'Crafty old devil.' The comment was automatic.

'That's why he's been so considerate all these weeks. He intends to see Jamie boy married off to Emily, take them both to California with him. He'll leave Tom Rennison here to run the unit, you see if I'm not right.' The entire hospital agreed.

James knew it, too. For Northiam had pointed out to him, kindly but firmly – it being, he implied, no more than his duty to bring unpalatable but inescapable facts to his junior's unwilling attention – that he hadn't a hope of achieving the post himself. Of course the selection board would assess him as fairly as anyone else, but he, Northiam, who had trained both young men, felt that in all honesty he must point out to James that Tom was the outstanding candidate. It would be morally wrong to allow James to suppose that he had a hope in hell of landing the job with Tom Rennison in the arena against him. 'Much better forget about it, come out with me to California, eh? I need you.' This, of course, was the underlying truth. In fact, as the Central agreed, he not only needed him, he was damn well going to have him. It was a safe bet that James Leyburn would be leaving for California with Northiam on the appointed date.

Like any other day, the day of the Appointment Board duly dawned.

Six carefully selected candidates presented themselves at the waiting room next door to the Board Room to be considered for the post of Director of the Cardio-Thoracic Unit at the Central London Hospital in succession to Marcus Northiam.

Tom Rennison was one of them. James Leyburn another. And as everyone had been predicting for weeks, it was a foregone conclusion. Each of them was interviewed. Tom Rennison, the same dark uncommunicative six-footer they remembered, was offered the post.

There were a number of other interviews scheduled for that day, for posts in the denuded cardio-thoracic unit, and candidates were pouring in and out from ten in the morning until six in the evening. They found themselves interviewed by their prospective chief, Rennison, sitting imperturbably on the Appointment Board, alongside Northiam.

James Leyburn, granite-faced, remote, impersonal, went back to work, took Northiam's afternoon follow-up clinic.

The following morning, though, he rang Charles Goring during surgery hours, made an appointment to see him that day.

'What did he want?' Valerie asked, told of the call as they drank mid-morning coffee together.

'To come and see me today.'

'What for?'

'He didn't say.' Charles, however, thought he knew. 'Could be he wants to ask for Emily's hand?'

Valerie was charmed. This, she agreed, was how marriages should be arranged.

'He was going to leave immediately after his morning round, and thought he'd arrive about one-thirty,' Charles added. 'He was emphatic that he wanted to talk to me before going out to see Em, so I said I'd give him a sandwich here.'

'I'll go to the delicatessen myself,' Valerie promised. 'And you'd better have a pot of real coffee.'

'Two or three sorts of sandwich, do you think? And perhaps some fruit. I suppose I'd better offer him a glass of sherry first.'

The meeting, however, turned out to be a long way from the celebration both the Gorings were anticipating. James had come to see Charles, he explained, because he wanted to go into Emily's exact physical condition.

Charles Goring was startled, wondered for a shocked moment or two if James didn't intend to marry his daughter unless he could give her a clean bill of health. 'Em is fully fit again,' he said somewhat stiffly, regarding him askance. 'I'm glad to say.'

'Good. Certainly she told me she was, but I wanted to be sure. A good deal depends on it. Because I've got to give her some news she may not care for, and I want to be certain she's fit to carry out the programme I'm proposing.' James was sombre, and Charles looked questioningly across his desk, found himself, to his astonishment, quietly praying that nothing was going to prevent the burly man with the faded blue eyes and gentle voice opposite him from becoming his son-in-law.

'Am I to be told what this is all about?'

'These are the facts.' James was abrupt. 'I'm remaining at the Central. But I'm sure Emily ought to go to the Ocean Hospital with Northiam. For a year, at any rate. And I'm going to do my best to insist that she does.'

Charles Goring stared. He didn't know where to begin. However, years of general practice asserted themselves, and he heard himself make an adequate start. 'First of all, you say you're remaining at the Central. Can I ask your reasons?'

'Not because I'm going to be given Northiam's post. Rennison's got that. I shall be working under him.'

'Is that a feasible proposition?'

For the first time since his arrival, James's face lifted into a spontaneous smile. 'Perfectly feasible,' he said, grinning like a boy. 'Northiam doesn't seem to believe it – or doesn't choose to believe it, more likely – but Tom and I have always been able to work together. There's no problem there.'

'You don't – er – forgive me – grudge him the post? Feel you should have been appointed?'

James shook his head. 'I'd like to have landed it, of course. Who wouldn't? But I knew if Tom really wanted it, he'd get it. He's streets ahead of the rest of us. But I also knew it would do me no harm to put in for it myself. And it hasn't. They've made me Assistant Director – feeling a bit guilty, you see, about not having given me the job when I'm there on the spot. Even Northiam wasn't able to stop them doing that, especially with Tom sitting there and backing me.'

'I see. It's none of my business, I know. But you are sure about this? You do know what you're doing? I mean, even if you did get on with Rennison in the old days, will it be the same as having him as your chief, instead of Northiam?'

James grinned again, just as happily. 'It'll be a damn sight better,' he said. 'Tom's a good bloke. We've worked together before. And the seniority business is nothing. Tom's always had the edge over me as a surgeon – people say so, and it's true. But what Northiam and the rest of them forget is that Tom and I haven't always been running neck and neck for the same post. I was still a student when Tom qualified. He's two years senior to me. Only two years, but it made a difference in those days. As a student, he taught me, and when I qualified and had my first job, he was my registrar. I took his advice then, and I see no reason why I shouldn't continue to take it now, when we're both ten years older.'

Charles was convinced. He believed every word of this. He could believe, too, that James, though he hadn't spelled this out quite so clearly, had had more than enough of Marcus Northiam. It was plain that if James was unhappy, it wasn't over the new set-up at the Central. And his next words bore this out.

'You know, I don't want to leave the Central,' he said. 'Northiam – and plenty of others, too – may think it a grotty old place, not what it was, a symbol of the deteriorating health service. But it's my hospital. I came to it raw from school, knowing nothing, and I'm sticking with it. I'd be thoroughly unhappy doing anything else.' He set his jaw, and Charles for the first time saw another facet of his personality. James was patient, kind and trustworthy, as everyone said. But he could also be implacable. 'To be fair to Northiam,' James was continuing, 'his decision is probably right for him. He's an innovator. He's already advanced the boundaries of achievement in chest and heart surgery, and given proper backing – which it's appallingly true to say he hasn't had in recent years at the Central – he'll continue to do so. He owes it to himself – and to suffering humanity, let's not blink it – to go where his outstanding gifts can be fully developed. That's for him. Fair enough. But it isn't for me. My place is at the Central.'

'I'm relieved to hear you say so. Personally, I think it's very sad about Northiam. A pity they didn't find some method of keeping him.'

Unexpectedly James's eyes danced. 'You may find that Tom and I don't do too badly by the old place, you know. We may achieve a few simple advances on our own account.'

Charles was highly embarrassed. 'I do apologise,' he began. 'I never meant to suggest – please don't think I – oh dear, I'm as bad as Bossy Brenda herself. What can I say?'

James shook his head. He was laughing. 'Forget it. Now, about Em. Never mind what I do, she ought to go with Northiam to the States. It's an opportunity it would be wrong for her to pass up, and least of all on my account.'

'All the same,' her father said, 'if you're staying here, I think she'll want to remain with you.'

'If she misses this chance, I'd never forgive myself. If her health is up to it, she ought to spend a year in the States at the minimum. How do you rate her health-wise?'

Charles told him, in considerable detail, taking out case-papers, showing him X-rays.

James listened, questioned, nodded. 'Then we're agreed,' he said finally. 'There's nothing to stop her taking off for the Ocean Hospital with Northiam next month. That's what I wanted to find out about. Now we must see she does it.'

'Are you sure you . . . ?'

'She has her life ahead of her, and I'm not standing by and watching her throw it away for my sake. I'm not going to tie her down in a marriage she may want now, but might live to regret.' He shivered. 'No, thanks very much. That I couldn't stand. I'd rather face it now, see her move on and live her life.'

'Don't be such a pessimist,' Charles said. 'No reason whatsoever that I can see why a marriage between you and Em shouldn't endure – and rather better than most, I'd hazard a guess.'

'What matters is that she's only eighteen. If she was, say, twenty-five or thereabouts and I was coming up to my forties, I don't think I'd worry so much.'

'I don't think you need worry at all. Personally, I hope very much she does settle down with you. I think she'll be a lucky girl. Possibly, though, you're right about the States. She ought to take up the opportunity, I suppose.' He sighed. 'It seems a long way away,' he added wistfully.

James echoed his sigh. 'It does.' His face was schooled, expressionless. 'However, I'll go along and sell her the idea.'

Charles saw him out to the Jaguar, returned to his consulting room and settled down to think matters out. James had a battle on his hands, he surmised. He began to feel a little more cheerful. As Emily's father, he was far from certain that James would get his way, and he found himself hoping that he wouldn't.

At this point in his cogitations Valerie came bursting in.

When was the wedding?

'When Em comes back from the States,' Charles said glumly, and told her what James had said.

Valerie was horrified. 'But Charles, Em is going to be heart-broken. Do you mean to say you simply sat here and let him – ?'

'I'm not sure that –'

'She's expecting to marry him before Christmas. You know it as well as I do. She may not have said so in so many words, but that's what she's planning for.'

'Yes, but – '

'You and James may have decided between you that your plan is all for Em's benefit, or some such rigmarole. But what she's going to feel when he puts it to her is that he's gone off her, he doesn't love her after all, and he's trying to get out of it.'

'But, Val, surely she must know by now that –'

'She'll imagine James is letting her down as gently as he can. She's so young, still. No girl of her age is as sure of herself as you seem to imagine. Honestly, you and James are as bad as each other. I'm sure you both meant well, but Em is going to be desolate. I'm going straight home to be with her, try to comfort her. After all, she isn't strong, she's been ill, and –'

'Fit as a flea now,' her father said brutally. He thought his wife was making heavy weather. 'Leave them alone. Let them work it out between themselves, Val.'

'You don't understand. I'm sorry, Charles, but you and the others will have to manage for yourselves this afternoon. Put the answering service on while you do your calls.' The door crashed behind her. The front door too. And then the door of her Mini in the drive banged, the car fired up, revved furiously, and she'd gone.

The drive from the town centre to Wistaria Lodge was short, and James, arguing with himself all the way, made it a brief fifteen minutes ahead of Valerie Goring.

Emily saw the car in the lane, ran out to meet him, and his arms, contrary to orders, went round her at once, and his lips found hers. Not exactly the planned preliminary to his rehearsed argument, and he broke away hastily and gave her his news.

He found she already knew a good deal of what he had to tell her. It had whizzed round the grapevine at the Central the previous day, and, that night, Mark Corrie, Wendy Stourbridge and Barbie Henderson had all rung Emily. She had had three more calls about it before lunch.

'So you're staying at the Central?' she asked. This was what her callers had not known – the thought that perhaps she'd have to ring them all back hovered, unwelcome, in her mind. They were all certain that having failed to land the Director's post, he'd be off to California in September. 'As Assistant Director? What does Northiam have to say to that?'

'He's put out, of course.' An understatement. Northiam had been not only shocked, but hurt, and James had seen it. In fact, the Central had always credited Northiam with more cold, crafty manipulation than was in him. He had, they were right, grown used to James. He did depend on him. He was also very fond of him and not only put out but unnerved and miserable at the prospect of going to a new hospital in a new country without him. 'He's only now beginning to grasp that I mean what I say – though I've been telling him since January. However, I didn't come to talk about myself. What's important is that you don't let this affect you. You must go out to California with him.'

'Me? Go with Northiam while you stay here? You must be joking.'

Conscientiously James began to remind her of the tremendous opportunities awaiting her, though how he was going to bear to part with her he couldn't imagine. Standing there arguing with him, in a brief slip of flower-printed cotton, tanned by the summer sun, long-legged and so beautiful he didn't know how to keep his hands off her, she was unforgettable, and he wanted only to keep her with him through all the hours there were.

'Look, James,' she was protesting. 'You can't honestly suppose I'm going to California without you, simply to look after Northiam, to run the office for that horrible old man when he's treated you so abominably – well, all I can say is, James, you must be out of your mind. Of course I shall stay here, if you aren't going. I was only going because of you.'

A sort of explosion of joy took place inside James. He'd never known anything like it. She was only going because of him. And that was the truth. He had to recognise it. He kissed her again.

Her response succeeded in startling him, and made nonsense of all his arguments. There might be a discrepancy in their ages, but there was no sign at all of any discrepancy in their loving. They belonged together.

At this inopportune moment, Valerie made an unappreciated entrance.

Emily and James sprang apart.

James embarked on some extraordinarily stilted conversation, while Emily scowled unlovingly at her mother.

Charles had been right, Valerie saw. Emily and James were capable of handling their own affairs. Embarrassed and at a loss, annoyed with herself too, her poise deserted her. All she had to do, as she realised afterwards, was walk straight out again. Instead, she dithered, gabbled a few unwanted clichés, finally heard herself offering, idiotically, tea and rock cakes.

James, hoping at least to have Emily to himself while Valerie went off to assemble these unwanted delicacies, accepted, Valerie departed at once, thankfully, to the kitchen and Emily melted satisfactorily into his arms again.

For about thirty seconds.

'Yoo-hoo! Yoo-hoo! Valerie! Val – er – ie! Where are you? Yoo-hoo!'

Fingers drummed on the window pane, and Brenda Langford-Thomas's large beaming face, wreathed as so often in self-congratulatory smiles, appeared. 'I saw the Mini,' she announced. 'So I knew – oh, it's you, Emily. Where's your mother? I thought, as she was at home, I'd pop in and sort out this problem over Wednesday's Meals-on-Wheels. I – now, I *know* you, don't I?'

'This is James Leyburn.' Emily filled in dutifully. 'From

the cardio-thoracic unit at the Central London Hospital. Mrs Langford-Thomas.'

'*Said* I knew you. Met at Christmas, didn't we? My husband was talking about you afterwards.' She nodded approvingly. James had made the grade.

'I'll tell Mother you're here,' Emily said.

Mrs Langford-Thomas stayed for tea, ate three rock cakes and explained to James how to run a Meals-on-Wheels service, as well as giving her husband's views on heart disease in old age, telling Valerie where she went wrong in the organisation of the practice and informing Emily she should take a job at the Royal Infirmary. 'Edward would find you one – expect you'd manage to make yourself useful.' She returned to James. 'What's all this about that fool Northiam going to the States?

'He leaves early in September,' James said crisply, an instant surge of loyalty to his chief taking possession of him. He stood up. 'I shall have to be getting back, Mrs Goring, I'm afraid. I've a dinner appointment, and I can't be late for it. Tom Rennison and Amyas Miller,' he added, for Emily's benefit. 'He's staying with us, thank the lord – to lend an air of respectability to the outfit.'

'Emily will see you off.' Valerie kept her head this time – but too late. 'More tea, Brenda?'

It didn't work. Brenda Langford-Thomas had never taken a hint, and she didn't make a start now.

'I'll come with you,' she told James. 'No, no more tea, thank you, Valerie. We've settled about Wednesday, haven't we? Where's your car, Mr Leyburn? Out this way, I expect. I shall tell Edward we had a talk.' Unstoppable, as always, she installed James in the Jaguar, shut the door on him. 'You know how to reach the motorway, do you?'

James said thank you, Mrs Langford-Thomas, he knew the way. 'I'll write,' he mouthed at Emily.

'Or telephone,' she said, a smile plastered implacably across her face, waving him off in a carefree manner. One thing she was determined not to do was to break down and howl out here in the road in front of Mrs Langford-Thomas.

Saved by the bell, James told himself. By a series of maddening accidents he'd succeeded in keeping to his decision to leave Emily free to go to California. The trouble was it didn't feel, any longer, like any sort of sensible decision. Difficult, in fact, to work out why he'd made it. And he'd never felt so lonely in his life.

The Jaguar nosed its way cautiously down the narrow winding lane, turned left into the road that led to the motorway.

And out of the hedge popped Emily. Red in the face, extremely untidy and rather twiggy, panting with the healthy lungs she owed to his and Northiam's skill.

James stalled the engine – something he'd never been known to do. His jaw dropped.

She opened the passenger door and fell in beside him. 'I'm coming with you,' she explained.

He stared at her, leant forward, picked a couple of twigs and an angry gesticulating spider out of her hair.

'Good,' he said, and put his arms round her.

THE END

EMILY by JILLY COOPER

If Emily hadn't gone to Annie Richmond's party, she would never have met the impossible, irresistible Rory Balniel – never have married him and been carried off to the wild Scottish island of Irasa to live in his ancestral home along with his eccentric mother Coco, and the dog, Walter Scott. She'd never have met the wild and mysterious Marina, a wraith from Rory's past, nor her brother, the disagreeable Finn Maclean; never have spent a night in a haunted highland castle, or been caught stealing roses in a see-through nightie . . . Yes, it all started at Annie Richmond's party . . .

'Emily opens windows on a new romantic landscape . . . The young and young-in-heart will revel in it.'

Newsagent and Bookshop

o 552 10277 6   60p

BELLA by JILLY COOPER

There was no doubt Bella Parkinson was a success: the most promising actress in London, bright, sexy – and hopelessly scatterbrained – she was taking the town by storm. Rupert Henriques, dashingly handsome and wealthy enough to buy her every theatre in London if she wanted it, couldn't wait to marry her . . .

But Bella had a secret in her past – and the one man who knew it was about to come into her life again . . . Rupert's sinister cousin Lazlo for some reason of his own, was trying to prevent her marriage. Before she knew where she was, Bella found herself in real danger . . .

o 552 10427 2   60p

BUSMAN'S HOLIDAY by LUCILLA ANDREWS

Discovering that the man she loved was already married was a shattering blow to Staff Nurse Frances Allendale. Not being one to make a scene, she nursed her bruised heart in secret and vowed that no man would ever have the chance to let her down again: months later, she still felt numb with the misery of it. Then, snatching a brief holiday with her aunt, she bumped into Dr David Loftus – and kept on bumping into him. Although she was on holiday, medical emergencies kept throwing them together, which was just what Frances didn't want. For although she admired his skill and his way with patients, in every action, every word of David's, she heard only an echo of the past.

0 552 10589 9   60p

ROMANTIC LADY by SYLVIA THORPE

There was to be an elopement.

Caroline Cresswell couldn't bear to see her friend, dearest Jenny, separated from her childhood sweetheart and forced into marriage with the odious Mr Ravenshaw. Jenny and Roland must elope and she, Caroline, would help . . .

It was exactly the kind of romantic adventure she needed to lift her spirits from the dull routine of a life looking after her uncle's children. She was twenty-seven, penniless, and had unfashionable red hair. Romance, for her, was participating in other people's lives. But she hadn't bargained for the elopement going wrong. Jenny and Roland got away all right, but Caroline found herself in a most dangerous predicament, and it was only the 'odious' Mr Ravenshaw who could help her . . .

0 552 10525 2   70p

CURTAIN FALL by JEAN URE

Six years ago, Nicola and David had been the brightest stars on the London ballet scene – the perfect partnership, both on stage and off. At the end of that one triumphant season Nicola had gone off to Australia on tour, where she had begun to hear vague rumours . . . David not dancing any more . . . David ill perhaps . . . And then the strange letter from David himself, telling her to forget him, to put him out of her life. She'd gone to Australia for four months – and stayed six years, eventually giving up dancing, giving up most things really, for without David, there didn't seem much point in going on. Now she was back in London, facing the hard slog back to fitness as a dancer – and forcing herself to face at last the mystery of what had happened to David . . .

0 552 10787 5   60p

HOSPITAL CALL by ELIZABETH HARRISON

Julie Alnaker was rich, young and lovely. She and Tony Grant, who'd recently qualified at the Central, had been childhood sweethearts, grown up together. But now Julie was engaged to Rubert Ferris, an eligible architect of whom even Julie's mother, the redoubtable Veronica, approved. Four days before the wedding, however, Julie was seriously injured in a riding accident. Toby, on call that day at the local hospital, was the first doctor to reach her, the first to realize that glowing, vital Julie might never walk again . . .

0 552 10104 4   45p

A SELECTED LIST OF CORGI ROMANCE
FOR YOUR READING PLEASURE

WHILE EVERY EFFORT IS MADE TO KEEP PRICES LOW, IT IS SOMETIMES
NECESSARY TO INCREASE PRICES AT SHORT NOTICE. CORGI BOOKS
RESERVE THE RIGHT TO SHOW AND CHARGE NEW RETAIL PRICES ON
COVERS WHICH MAY DIFFER FROM THOSE ADVERTISED IN THE TEXT
OR ELSEWHERE.

THE PRICES SHOWN BELOW WERE CORRECT AT THE TIME OF GOING TO
PRESS (FEBRUARY 79)

☐ 10589 9	BUSMAN'S HOLIDAY	*Lucilla Andrews*	60p
☐ 10590 2	NURSE ERRANT	*Lucilla Andrews*	50p
☐ 10786 7	NO ESCAPE FROM LOVE	*Barbara Cartland*	50p
☐ 10602 X	PUNISHMENT OF A VIXEN	*Barbara Cartland*	50p
☐ 10549 X	DUEL WITH DESTINY	*Barbara Cartland*	50p
☐ 10543 0	THE HUNDREDTH CHANCE	*Ethel M. Dell*	60p
☐ 10588 0	THE WAY OF AN EAGLE	*Ethel M. Dell*	60p
☐ 10560 0	THE REASON WHY	*Elinor Glyn*	60p
☐ 10638 0	DANGEROUS CALL NO 10	*Elizabeth Harrison*	50p
☐ 10548 1	THE SILVER ROSE BOWL	*Cathy Linton*	50p
☐ 10278 4	SISTER IN WAITING	*Cathy Linton*	45p
☐ 10428 0	RICHMOND HERITAGE	*Susan Sallis*	60p
☐ 10525 2	ROMANTIC LADY	*Sylvia Thorpe*	70p
☐ 10383 7	EARLY STAGES (RIVERSIDE ROMANCE NO 1)	*Jean Ure*	50p
☐ 10384 5	ALL IN A SUMMER SEASON (RIVERSIDE ROMANCE NO 2)		
		Jean Ure	50p

*All these books are available at your bookshop or newsagent; or can be ordered direct from the
publisher. Just tick the titles you want and fill in the form below.*

CORGI BOOKS, Cash Sales Department, P.O. Box 11, Falmouth, Cornwall.

Please send cheque or postal order, no currency.

U.K. send 22p for the first book plus 10p per copy for each additional book ordered to a
maximum charge of 82p to cover the cost of postage and packing.

B.F.P.O and Eira allow 22p for the first book plus 10p per copy for the next 6 books,
thereafter 4p per book.

Overseas customers please allow 30p for the first book and 10p per copy for each
additional book.

NAME (block letters) ....

ADDRESS ....

FEBRUARY 1979 ....